PONY CLUB SECRETS

Destiny
and the
Wild Horses

The Pony Club Secrets series:

Also available:

PONY CLUB SECRETS

Destiny
and the
Wild Horses

Stacy Gregg

HarperCollins *Children's Books*

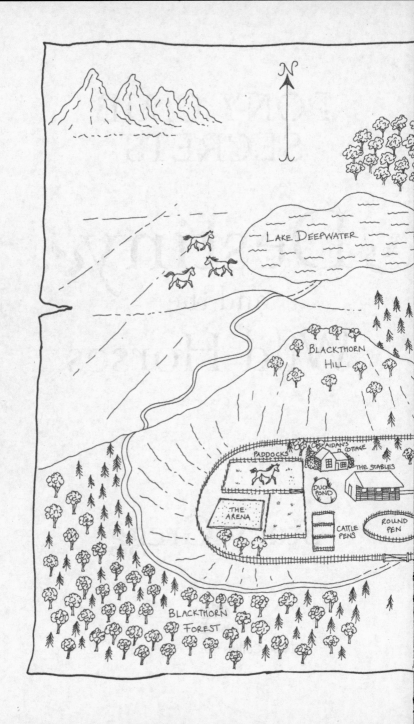

For my mum, who never liked horses
at all, but loved her two horse-mad
daughters. Thanks for everything.

www.stacygregg.co.uk

First published in Great Britain by HarperCollins *Children's Books* in 2008
HarperCollins *Children's Books* is a division of HarperCollins*Publishers* Ltd
1 London Bridge Street, London, SE1 9GF
This edition published in 2015

www.harpercollins.co.uk

ISBN-13 978-0-00-724518-5

Printed and bound by CPI Group (UK) Ltd, Croydon, CR0 4YY

CHAPTER 1

One of the best feelings in the world is waking up and thinking, *Ohmygod, I'm late for school!* That isn't the good bit obviously. The good bit comes in a sudden rush a few seconds later when you realise that you don't have to go to school after all because today isn't an ordinary Monday – it's the first day of the summer holidays!

Issie was savouring that exact moment right now as she lay snuggled up in bed. She gave her legs a big, wriggly stretch underneath the duvet. There was something so luxurious about lying there, knowing that she didn't have to hurry up and put her uniform on and pack her book bag. No school for two whole months. And this summer promised to be the best ever.

Issie had big plans for the holidays. And most of those

plans involved Blaze, her chestnut Anglo-Arab mare. Summer meant pony-club season. There would be gymkhanas, ribbon days and one-day events to ride, and Issie had Blaze in perfect condition ready f or competition.

Her pony had been schooling beautifully ever since Issie got her back from Francoise D'arth. They had been having regular dressage lessons with Tom Avery and she was amazed at how responsive and clever her horse was. Now that Issie and Tom knew Blaze's real background – that she had once been part of a famous troupe of dancing Arabians – they had begun to try new things with her. Under Avery's tutelage, Blaze and Issie had easily mastered fancy moves like shoulder-ins and piaffes.

"That mare is the perfect school mistress for you," Avery told her. "We're going to make huge strides in your training this summer, Issie."

Avery was confident that Blaze was ready to compete in the summer series dressage competitions at the Chevalier Point Pony Club which began that weekend. "You'll only be in the novice section so there certainly wouldn't be any piaffes in your dressage test," he said.

Still, Issie was nervous. She had never done dressage on Blaze before. What if the mare got all heated up and panicked in the arena? What if she forgot the test and got lost halfway through?

"Don't be ridiculous!" Stella had told Issie when she blabbed her fears. "You and Blaze have practised your test, like, at least twenty times! I still don't know it and Coco is being so stubborn lately she won't even lead on the correct leg when she canters. She's being a total nightmare!"

With the competition looming, Stella, Issie and Kate all agreed that they needed more dressage practice, so Tom Avery had arranged a training session for the Chevalier Point riders at the pony club that morning.

Issie gave one last squirm under the duvet. It was so warm and comfy she still didn't want to get up. "One, two, three!" she counted herself out of bed, jumping up on three and making a dash across the bedroom to the pile of washing on the floor. She pulled on her jodhpurs and grabbed a hair band off her dresser, sweeping her long, straight, dark hair back in a ponytail as she headed down the stairs.

Her mother had left for work early that morning but she had left Issie a note on the kitchen table.

Gone to work (obviously!). Have to pick up groceries on the way home so won't be back until six. We need to talk about the holidays – make sure you are home by seven for dinner. Mum x

Issie read the note, popped two slices of wholegrain bread in the toaster and poured herself a glass of orange juice from the fridge.

What did her mum mean "We need to talk about the holidays"? Her holidays were already decided – she planned to spend every minute at pony club with Stella, Kate, Dan and Ben. What else was there to talk about?

After a second round of toast she finished getting dressed, grabbed her bike out of the garage and cycled off to pony club.

When Issie arrived at the club she found her two best friends Stella and Kate staring at an expensive-looking silver and blue horse truck that had just pulled up at the club grounds.

"Wow! Very flashy," said Kate.

"I've never seen that truck before. It doesn't belong to any of the Chevalier Point riders, does it?" Stella asked. Her question was answered instantly as a girl with a sour expression and two ramrod-straight shiny blonde plaits emerged from the truck to open the gates.

"I should have known! Stuck-up Tucker's mummy has bought her a brand new horse truck," Stella sighed.

They watched as Natasha stood sulking beside the truck, refusing to move until her mum asked her for a third time to help lower the ramp. Issie had been expecting to see Natasha's palomino mare Goldrush coming down the ramp. Instead the girl led out a very refined-looking rose-grey with a white heart shape on his forehead and a steel-grey mane and tail. He wore a dark navy wool rug and matching floating boots to protect his delicate legs. As Natasha removed the boots the girls saw that his hind legs had two pretty white socks.

"Check out Natasha's new horse!" Stella gave a low whistle of admiration.

"Issie! You have to go and ask her about it!" Kate demanded.

"What? Why me?" Issie groaned. "Natasha can't stand me!"

"At least she speaks to you! She won't even bother

to talk to me or Kate," Stella countered. "Go on! Go and ask her."

"All right, all right…" Issie muttered as she walked off across the paddock. The truth was, she didn't need much coaxing. She was dying to know about the new horse too.

"Hi, Natasha, I didn't know you were riding with us today," Issie said.

"Hmmph? Oh hello, Isabella," Natasha said.

"It's Isadora," Issie replied flatly. One of Natasha's favourite games was to accidentally-on-purpose forget Issie's name.

"What-ever," Natasha sniffed. "How's your little circus pony?"

Ever since Issie had beaten Natasha Tucker at the pony-club one-day event, the bratty blonde had been spiteful towards Issie and her chestnut mare. Natasha had called Blaze a "scruffy pit pony with no papers" until the truth about Blaze was discovered: she had once been one of the El Caballo Danza Magnifico mares, the famous Anglo-Arabs with immaculate bloodlines dating back to the great desert-bred Arabians.

Of course even this news didn't stop Natasha. Now that everyone knew just how valuable Blaze's breeding really was, Natasha had taken to teasing Issie about having a "circus pony", even though everyone knew that the El Caballo Danza Magnifico wasn't a circus at all – it was a *haute ècole* riding school that travelled the world performing fantastic dressage movements to music. Blaze had once been the star of the school. But now, thanks to a mysterious benefactor, the chestnut mare belonged to Issie.

"Blaze is fine thanks, Natasha," Issie said. She turned her attention to the beautiful rose-grey gelding. "Is this your new horse? What happened to Goldrush?"

"I told Mummy that Goldrush simply wasn't up to my level any more so we got rid of her," Natasha said coolly. "This is Fabergé. He's a sport horse, bred by Iggy Dalrymple, so you can just imagine how much he cost us. Mummy says it's vulgar to talk about money but she did tell me that he cost more than all of her Prada handbags put together."

"He's really beautiful," Issie said as she ran her hand gently down the crest of Fabergé's neck. "Are you going to enter him in the summer dressage series?"

"Uh-huh. I'd say we're bound to win it actually." Natasha smirked. "Fabergé has been off at Ginty McLintoch's stables for two weeks being schooled up. Ginty herself has put in hours of work on him – Mummy paid her an absolute bomb to do it." Natasha wrinkled up her nose. "I couldn't be bothered with doing all that training myself! Anyway, now he is positively a push-button ride apparently. I can just sit there and Fabergé knows exactly what to do. It should be a piece of cake to win the novice ring this season."

"Well, I guess we'll see you at the dressage test on Saturday," Issie said. "Blaze and I are in the novice ring too." Issie was sure she saw the smug look on Natasha's face fade for a moment. And then the blonde regained her haughty composure.

"They don't give you points for doing circus tricks in proper dressage, you know."

"That's a pity because Blaze can balance a ball on her nose while doing a dance on her hind legs," said a voice behind them.

Issie turned round to see Stella on top of Coco, smiling brightly at her. Kate, who was with her on Toby, was trying to suppress her giggles. Natasha's scowl deepened.

"You always have your little gang with you to stick up for you, don't you?" Natasha snapped. "I wonder how cool you'd be if you were all on your own with no one else to look after you."

They were interrupted at that moment by Tom Avery's booming voice.

"Riders into the arena now, please!" he instructed.

Issie gave the rose-grey gelding a pat. "Anyway, it was nice to meet you, Fabergé," she said. Natasha continued to glare at her. "Bye, Natasha." Issie shrugged and began to run back across the paddock to the tethering rail where Blaze was waiting for her.

"Can we all line up, please?" Tom Avery said.

The riders had been warming up their ponies. Dan and Ben had arrived a little late, but had quickly tacked up Kismit and Max and joined the others. Now the six riders all stood in the centre of the arena awaiting Avery's instructions.

Avery slapped his riding crop against his long brown leather boots to get their attention. "With the dressage test approaching this weekend, I think you're all ready for some more advanced schooling," he said. "Does anyone here know how to do a flying change?"

Without hesitation a hand shot up amongst the riders.

"Ah, Natasha. Of course. Please come forward for a moment," Avery said. Natasha cast a glance at Issie as she rode Fabergé past her to stand at the front of the ride.

"Now Natasha here is going to demonstrate a flying change," Avery said. As you all know, a flying change is when we ask our horse to canter with a leading leg, and then we ask with our aids and make the horse change legs in midair." Avery paused. "You might have seen this on your Olympic dressage videos at home. It looks a bit like the horse is skipping, doesn't it?"

"Anky makes it look really easy when she does it on Bonfire," Stella said.

"Well then, let's see how easy it really is, shall we?" Avery said. "Natasha, why don't you work your horse around the arena at a canter and then ride a flying change through the middle of the school to show us how it's done?"

Natasha set off on Fabergé with a look of grim determination on her face. She cantered the rose-grey around the arena and then turned him down the centre of the school to begin her flying change. In the middle of the school Natasha gave Fabergé a big kick with her heels. Nothing happened. She looked exasperated. Poor Fabergé looked confused.

"Try again, this time with nice, clear aids. You don't need to kick your horse! Just put that right leg forward on the girth," Avery instructed. Natasha rode around and down the centre line again. This time, though, she ignored Avery's advice and gave Fabergé an almighty boot with her right leg. Fabergé shot up like a rocket, putting in a vigorous buck. Natasha gave a yelp of horror as she flew over Fabergé's head and sailed through the air, coming down in a heap on the sandy surface of the arena. Fabergé gave a terrified snort and cantered off. Dan and Ben quickly clucked their horses and rode after him while Natasha stood up grumpily and dusted herself down.

"Are you all right?" Avery asked her. Natasha, who was bright red in the face, nodded quietly.

"He's a very sensitive horse. If I were you I'd master the basics on him before you try a flying change again," Avery said kindly. Then he gestured to Issie. "Isadora, why don't you give it a try on Blaze? Remember, you need to move your right leg to the girth."

"Good girl, c'mon," Issie clucked to Blaze as she set off around the perimeter of the arena. As she rode down the centre line in a canter she sat tall in the saddle and tried to think about arranging her legs into the correct position. Right in the middle of the arena Issie did exactly as Avery had instructed – she moved one leg forward and the other leg back and squeezed hard. Beneath her she felt Blaze rise up and throw out her front legs like a schoolgirl skipping down the street – a flying change!

"Textbook stuff! A very nicely executed flying

change." Avery was pleased. "Excellent. Now, who's going to give it a go next? Dan? How about you?"

Issie slowed Blaze down to a walk and gave her a big slappy pat on the neck as she took her place back in the line. "Not bad for a circus pony!" she whispered to her pony.

In the end, Issie was the only rider that day to master the flying change. "It's not as easy as it looks," Stella had grumbled as they untacked the ponies. Issie had nodded in agreement with her friend, but the truth was that to her it had been easy. It was as if she only had to think about what she wanted to do and Blaze would respond. OK, so there weren't any fancy flying changes in their dressage test this weekend. Still, Issie felt certain for the first time ever that she and Blaze stood a really good chance. They might even win.

"Mum! I'm home! I did a flying change today!" Issie charged in through the front door without pausing to take off her riding boots.

"Isadora! You'd better not still have your muddy boots on!" her mother yelled back from the kitchen.

Issie stopped dead and ran back to the laundry, stripping off her boots and socks before running back to the kitchen to find her mother.

"You can tell me all about it while you eat your dinner," Mrs Brown said. And so, between mouthfuls of potato salad, Issie told her mum about Natasha and the flying changes and the dressage series that was starting on Saturday.

"Blaze is going so perfectly. This is going to be the best summer I've ever had!" Issie said.

Mrs Brown didn't say anything. She just looked down at her plate and gave her quiche a distracted poke with her fork.

"Mum? What's wrong? You've hardly said anything since I got home," Issie said.

Mrs Brown pushed her plate aside. She looked serious, but still she didn't speak.

"Mum?"

"Issie, I am afraid I've got some, well, it's not bad news really. I mean it's good but it's not good…" Mrs Brown hesitated. "I've been invited away on a conference for work. They're going to fly me there and pay for accommodation – the whole thing. I'll be gone for two weeks."

"That's great!" Issie said. "When?"

"We leave on Friday," Mrs Brown said. "That's why I wanted to talk to you tonight about the holidays. I've made plans for you."

"What do you mean?" Issie said.

"Sweetie, I can't leave you here by yourself. If I'm away for two weeks then who would look after you? You're only thirteen. You're not old enough to be by yourself."

"Cool. I can go stay with Stella!" Issie said.

Mrs Brown shook her head. "There's something else, Issie. I got a phone call last night from your Aunt Hester. It turns out she's had a bad fall off one of her silly horses and broken her leg."

"Aunty Hess? That's terrible! Is she OK?"

"She's fine," Mrs Brown sighed, "but she can't possibly look after that farm of hers. She has Aidan to help her but it's not enough…" Mrs Brown paused "… and so I suggested that you could go and stay with her until she gets better again."

"Me?" Issie squawked.

"Sweetie – it's perfect! You can stay with Hester while I'm away, and she needs your help so it suits her," Mrs Brown explained. "Besides, you've never been to the farm before and I know you will just love it. Hester has loads of ponies and all those other animals that she trains. You'll adore it there."

"But, Mum! Blaze and I have been working so hard for the dressage competition," Issie said.

"I know, honey. But I can't see any other way." Mrs Brown sighed. "I've already asked Aidan if he can drive through to get you. He's going to be here on Wednesday morning."

"But it's Monday now! When were you going to tell me this? What about Stella and Kate? What about my holidays? What about Blaze?"

"I'm sorry, Issie. It's the only option. Really, you'll see. You're going to love it at the farm… Issie? Issie!"

But Issie didn't hear her. She had already left the kitchen in tears, run up the stairs to her bedroom and slammed the door shut behind her.

CHAPTER 2

How could the school holidays go so wrong so fast? Issie flung herself down on her bed and buried her face deep in the duvet. She couldn't believe her mum would ruin her summer like this!

"Issie? Come on. Let me in and let's talk about this," Mrs Brown's voice echoed softly outside Issie's bedroom door.

Issie stood up and walked over to let her mother in, before flopping back down, rather over-dramatically, with her face in the duvet again.

"It's not fair. Why do I have to go to Aunty Hester's?" She gave a muffled groan from beneath the blankets.

"Sweetie, I really do think it's the best idea for everyone – especially Aunty Hess," Mrs Brown said.

"It would be a huge favour to her if you helped out until her leg is better. Hess has a big movie coming up. They start filming in a couple of months and she has dozens of animals that need to be trained. She has so much work to do she could really use an extra pair of hands…"

"But *I* had plans!" Issie said. "The dressage series is on and Blaze is going so well. I can't just leave her and go away to the farm."

Mrs Brown suddenly perked up. "Hey! I tell you what – how about if you could take Blaze with you?"

"What do you mean?"

"You could take Blaze to Aunty Hester's. I could call Aidan and ask him to bring the horse truck when he comes to pick you up on Wednesday and then you can take Blaze with you. I'm sure Hess won't mind. One more horse on that enormous farm of hers won't make the slightest difference."

Issie sat up. "Do you mean it? Could Blaze really come too?"

"I don't see why not," Mrs Brown said. She was clearly very pleased with herself for coming up with the idea. "You know what? I'm going to give Hess a call now and ask her!"

Mrs Brown trotted off down the stairs and a moment

later Issie could hear her on the phone chatting and laughing happily with her sister.

If I could take Blaze with me, Issie thought, *maybe it wouldn't be so bad.*

Issie really liked her aunt. For starters, Hester was horsy through and through. Issie always thought it was so unfair that her own mother hated horses while her Aunt Hess adored them. If Aunt Hester had been her mother then she would have got a pony straight away. Instead she had to beg for years before her mum finally gave in and bought Mystic.

Mrs Brown couldn't understand why Issie loved horses so much. "It must be genetic. Your aunt was exactly the same when she was your age," Mrs Brown had told Issie on more than one occasion. "Hess was totally horse-mad! And now look at her – she has seven horses, a trained pig, a goat, several sheep, those nuisance blasted dogs and heaven knows what else on that crazy farm of hers!"

Hester worked as an animal trainer for the movies. Three years ago she decided to set up her own business, and so she bought Blackthorn Farm, where she kept and trained her menagerie of four-legged movie stars.

Blackthorn Farm was a rambling old country manor, high up in the hills near Gisborne. The manor and grounds had once been quite grand, apparently, but Hester had got the place for very little because it had become quite rundown.

Blackthorn Manor was huge – it had eleven bedrooms – but Hester lived there alone. She had been married three times – "All of them wonderful weddings!" she told Issie – but she had never had any children of her own. She called Issie her "favourite niece" which was a bit of a joke between the two of them since Issie was in fact her only niece.

Hester ran the farm herself with help from her young stable manager, Aidan. With her leg in plaster and all those animals to look after, she was bound to need some extra help.

Issie listened to her mum hang up the receiver and head back up the stairs. When she entered Issie's room she had an enormous smile on her face.

"Good news! Hess says she'd love to meet your horse, Issie. It all sounds perfect. There's a spare stall for Blaze in the stable complex and she's getting it ready for your arrival and Aidan will be here to pick you both up first thing on Wednesday morning with the truck. It's a long drive. It will probably take you most of the day to get there."

"Really? So Blaze can come with me? And we're actually going?" Issie said.

Mrs Brown looked at her daughter's uncertain expression. "Issie? I thought that would make you happy. You can take Blaze with you – there's lots of land to ride there – that farm is positively huge – you could ride all day without leaving the property."

"I know… I mean, yes, it's great, Mum. Honestly. And I want to go and help out Aunty Hess and everything…" Issie sighed. "It's just that Stella and Kate and me had the whole summer planned out and now I'm not going to be here. And what about Tom? He was expecting me to ride the dressage series and—"

"I'm sure Stella and Kate will understand. I know you three are pretty hard to separate but maybe it will be nice to have some time on your own for once," Mrs Brown said. "As for Tom, you leave him to me. I'm sure he'll agree with me that a few weeks out of your training schedule isn't going to ruin your chances of riding at Badminton!"

"Mum! As if!" Issie laughed.

"Aha! I knew I could get you smiling again." Mrs Brown grinned back at her daughter. "Now, I'll dig out your suitcase and let's make sure you actually have some clean clothes to pack, shall we? Hand me that pile of washing over there and we'll get started!"

The news that Issie was going to Blackthorn Farm left Stella speechless – for a moment anyway. "Stella?" Issie said. There was silence at the other end of the phone and then a torrent of words came pouring out.

"I can't believe your mum is doing this! We had plans, Issie! Big plans! What about the dressage series? What about the summer holidays? It's not fair! How long will you be gone for?"

"I don't know. I suppose I'll stay there until Aunt Hester's leg is better and she can manage on her own again." Issie sighed. "You know, I am her favourite niece and everything."

"Very funny, Issie! Your mum's ruined our whole summer! Have you told Kate yet?"

"No," Issie said, "I thought I'd tell you first because I knew you'd take it so well!"

Stella gave a giggle at this. "You're right, I am overreacting, aren't I? You might only be gone for a couple of weeks. I suppose we can always email each other while you're away."

"Actually I don't even know if Aunty Hess has email.

Blackthorn Farm is in the middle of nowhere. Aidan is coming to pick me up first thing on Wednesday morning and it will take us pretty much all day to drive there."

"Who's Aidan?" Stella said.

"He works for Aunty Hess. He runs her stables and he's driving the horse truck down from the farm to pick up me and Blaze."

"Oooh! How old is Aidan? What does he look like?"

"What? Oh, Stella! I think he's, like, maybe seventeen. I have no idea what he looks like. I've never been to the farm so I've never met him, OK?" Issie snapped. Stella had gone a bit boy-mad lately, which Issie found very annoying. She hadn't even thought about what Aidan might be like – but now she realised he would be here tomorrow and they would have to spend the whole day together driving to the farm.

"I'd better tell Dan. I'm sure that will make him jealous," Stella laughed.

"Stella! Don't!" Issie said.

Dan had asked Issie out once – at least she thought he'd asked her out – but things got all confused because it turned out he'd asked Natasha too and maybe it had never been a date. Anyway it was all a big mess and nothing had ever happened after that.

Issie sighed. "Oh, go on then. Tell Dan and Ben that I've gone away and tell Natasha too while you're at it; I'm sure she'll be thrilled that I won't be competing against her in the dressage."

Stella groaned. "Ohmygod! Natasha. I'd forgotten about that. She's going to be unbearable if she wins. Issie! How can you leave me? Don't go!"

"I'm hanging up now, Stella," Issie said. "I have to go pack and then I have to clean Blaze's tack and get her floating boots out and make sure that all her gear is ready to go…"

"OK, OK." Stella sighed. "But you'd better email me. And if they have no email then send a carrier pigeon or whatever they've got up there."

"Knowing Aunty Hess, I wouldn't be surprised if she hasn't trained up a pigeon or two," Issie giggled. "It's a deal – I'll send you a letter by pigeon post."

Aidan was due to arrive at seven a.m. on Wednesday morning to pick Issie up. But when Issie opened her curtains at six a.m. to check the weather, she saw the horse truck was already parked outside.

"Mum?" she called out as she padded downstairs, still in her pyjamas. "The horse truck is here already."

"I know," her mother replied from the kitchen. "Come in and meet Aidan!"

Issie walked through to find her mother making coffee for a young boy in a plaid shirt and jeans who was sitting at the table. The boy, who looked not that much older than Issie, had black hair that fell over his face in a long, floppy fringe almost covering his eyes. He stood up as Issie sat down next to him and stuck out his hand for her to shake.

"Hi," he said, "I'm Aidan."

"Hello Issie! I mean… hello, I'm Issie!" Issie said, flustered. She shook Aidan's hand. "Sorry, I'm not ready to go yet obviously," she said, looking down at her pyjamas, which she now realised were the ones with pink kittens all over them. "I didn't expect you to get here so early."

"I got here late last night and slept in the horse truck," Aidan said.

"Was that uncomfortable?" Mrs Brown asked.

"It's better than my bed back at the farm!" Aidan grinned. "It might look like a horse truck on the outside, but the inside is pure luxury. Hester's got it rigged up with two beds and a shower so we can travel with the horses. There's a kitchen too," he added, "but I never use it. I'm not a very good cook."

"Well, don't you worry about that, I'll make you breakfast." Mrs Brown smiled.

"Thanks, that would be great." Aidan grinned.

He looked over at Issie, who was fidgeting and looking down at the table, clearly embarrassed to be meeting a boy for the first time dressed in her pussycat pyjamas. Mrs Brown noticed her daughter shifting uncomfortably in her chair. "Issie, it will take a few minutes to get breakfast sorted. Why don't you go and have a shower and get dressed and I'll call you when it's ready?" she suggested.

"Thanks, Mum!" Issie said gratefully.

When she came downstairs for the second time that morning, Issie was ready to go. She was wearing her favourite jeans, a pair of brown leather boots and her favourite T-shirt. Her long dark hair was now neatly combed and tied back in a thick ponytail. She carried a big overnight bag thrown over one shoulder and was dragging a suitcase with her right hand.

"Let me help you." Aidan smiled, taking the bags off her. "I'll put these in the truck." He went out the front door with Issie's bags and she sat down at the table as her mum dished up her bacon and eggs.

"Aidan's already eaten. You finish up and then you can get going," Mrs Brown said as she poured herself a coffee from the plunger and sat down next to Issie. "Aidan will help you load Blaze at the pony club and then you can set off straight from there. Aunt Hess is expecting you in time for tea. I've packed you a banana cake to take with you; Hess is terrible at baking. In fact, all her cooking is terrible! You'll probably come back as skinny as a rake!" Mrs Brown said. She gave Issie a big hug.

"I've packed you a big bag of carrots for Blaze too in case she gets hungry during the trip."

Issie smiled. "Thanks, Mum!" she said.

"Take care, honey. Call me every night, OK?" Mrs Brown was still hugging Issie.

"Mum, you have to let go of me now, I need to leave." Issie laughed.

"Are we ready to go?" Aidan stuck his head around the kitchen door. "The truck is all packed. Let's go get this horse of yours."

It was only a five minute drive to the pony club, and Issie said nothing all the way. She was quiet even as she velcroed on Blaze's floating boots and loaded the dainty chestnut mare into the truck stall, tying her up with a hay net for the journey.

Issie hopped back into the cab, Aidan raised the ramp and they drove out through the pony-club gates. Issie took one last look over her shoulder at the horses who were left behind grazing happily. "Bye, Toby. Bye, Coco," she murmured. She felt a strange sensation in her tummy, like the butterfly nerves she usually got before a showjumping competition. She looked back through the window of the cab. Blaze was chewing contentedly on her hay net. Issie pressed her nose up against the glass and gazed at her pony, taking in the delicate dish of her nose and the deep, dark eyes fringed by her flaxen forelock.

"She's beautiful, isn't she?" Aidan said.

"What?"

"Your mare." Aidan smiled at Issie. "An Anglo-Arab, right? Half Arab and half Thoroughbred?"

"Uh-huh," Issie said.

"She looks like a very special horse. Where did you get her?" Aidan asked.

"It's a long story," Issie said.

"It's a long drive too," Aidan smiled, "so why don't you start now and maybe you'll be finished by the time we get there."

Issie laughed. "OK," she said. And so she told Aidan the story of Blaze. She started right at the very beginning, from the awful tragedy of Mystic's death. When she had lost her lovely grey gelding she thought she could never love another horse again. And then Avery had turned up with Blaze. She had been rescued by the International League for the Protection of Horses and was in a desperate state, terrified and half-starved. It had taken every last ounce of love that Issie had in her to win Blaze's trust and bring her back again. She nearly lost Blaze once more when Francoise D'Arth arrived in Chevalier Point and told her that Blaze was actually one of the famed El Caballo Danza Magnifico Arabians.

"She must be worth a fortune!" Aidan said.

Issie nodded. "I guess so. I don't really know. When Francoise brought Blaze back to me she told me that someone had paid for Blaze and wanted to give her to me. Now she's mine to keep for ever. I never found out who it was or how much they paid for her – and since I'll never, ever sell her I guess it doesn't really matter how much she is worth."

Aidan looked at Issie. "You've been through a lot with this mare, haven't you? I can see why you didn't want to leave her behind."

"She's my best friend." Issie smiled.

Aidan was right: it was a long drive to the farm. They made their way out of the city into the open countryside, and it was late in the afternoon when they drove up to the crest of a very high hill and Aidan finally turned the truck down the driveway that led to the farm. The limestone driveway seemed to almost burrow a tunnel through the dense native woods that surrounded them. The trees blocked out the light above them and Issie could hear scraping and rustling as the enormous branches that hung overhead began to brush against the roof of the horse truck. She pushed her nose up against the passenger window and stared out at the lush ferns, bright vermillion fuchsias, brilliant yellow kowhai flowers and boughs of crab apples laden with blood-red fruit. When the truck finally emerged into the golden afternoon light she found herself in front of an enormous two-storey white mansion, with latticed Victorian verandas and broad balconies on the second floor. There were cherry trees in full bloom covering the vast circular lawn in front of the house.

Standing in the middle of the lawn under the cherry trees was Aunty Hess. She wore a long, white, cotton dress and her hair, which was very blonde and tightly curled, tumbled over her shoulders. There was a loud baying as three dogs came bounding out of the house to join her. One was a smiling golden retriever, the other was an enormous black shaggy Newfoundland and the third was a whippet-thin black and white hound.

As they drove up towards the manor the dogs all leapt up dangerously, bouncing up to put their paws on the side of the horse truck as it pulled to a stop in front of the cherry trees. Then they dashed off again at a mad run and sat obediently on either side of the woman in the white cotton dress.

"Lie down, stay," Hess instructed the dogs. All three of them put their heads on their paws and lay perfectly still as she walked towards the horse truck and opened Issie's passenger door.

"Aunty Hess!" Issie beamed down at her aunt.

"Isadora! My favourite niece!" Hess held her arms up to help her down from the truck cab. "Welcome to Blackthorn Farm."

CHAPTER 3

Aunt Hester led Issie through the cherry trees and up the wide path that led to the grand entrance of Blackthorn Manor.

"You must be starving after driving all day!" she said. "Don't worry about your pony; Aidan will take the truck down and settle her in at the stables. You come with me. I've made you dinner."

Dinner, it turned out, was three burnt fish fingers with runny mashed potato and peas. "Your mother probably told you that my cooking isn't up to much," Hester smiled, "and I can tell you that she's quite right and it really hasn't improved!"

While Issie ate, Hester sat down next to her with her leg propped up on a chair. Issie hadn't noticed at first, but under that white cotton dress Hester was sporting a brilliant pink plaster cast that ran from her toes to her knee.

"Wow!' Issie said.

"Pretty, isn't it?" Hester smiled, knocking on the plaster with her knuckles. "They let me choose the colour, you know. Schiaparelli pink is so chic, don't you think? I'm still supposed to use crutches but I can't be bothered so I use a walking stick or I sometimes just hop," Hester continued. "It's a very long driveway down to the stables when you're hopping on one foot, I can tell you. And feeding out the farm animals takes me for ever."

"How did it happen, Aunty Hess?"

"Oh, I was training one of the horses, Diablo. I was teaching him to lie down dead as if he had been shot, you see, like in a cowboy movie. Well, he lay down dead all right, but he did it right on top of me! Not his fault, of course; he was only doing what I asked him to do. But it broke my leg in two places, and there you go!" Aunt Hester smiled. "I must say it is lovely to have my favourite niece and her mystery mare here to help me out."

"Blaze! I should go and check on her." Issie suddenly panicked. "She's not used to being stabled and she doesn't know any of your horses. I should—"

"Don't worry about Blaze," Aunt Hester reassured her.

"Aidan will take excellent care of her. He used to work at a fancy stable in Ireland when he wasn't much older than you are now – looking after racehorses for some high and mighty Arab Sultan. It was all rather grand. Frightfully expensive horses too! I'm sure looking after your pony is well within his capabilities. We'll go down there in just a moment and you can check on her. But first..." Aunt Hester swept her hand dramatically towards the doorway that led to the main hall "...the grand tour!"

"Downstairs to start with, I think," Hester said. "Yes, yes. Follow me." She led Issie through a maze of vast wood-panelled rooms, each one more fantastic than the last, all of them with high ceilings, well-worn parquet floors and enormous, sparkling crystal chandeliers. The walls, which were papered in faded flock wallpaper, were adorned with antlers and wild boar heads. There were paintings everywhere of elegant racehorses and black and white photographs of grand old ladies looking out at you regally from the frame.

"Not my taste, you understand," Hester giggled. "I'm a little more shabby chic, aren't I, darling? Most of this lot was already here when I arrived. They sold the place to me lock, stock and barrel," she said, sweeping through the billiard room, where a game of pool was set up under the watchful gaze of two large stuffed pheasants.

Hester set a cracking pace through the manor. Issie had thought the plaster cast would have slowed her aunt down, but she grasped herself a walking cane out of the wicker basket in the hallway, propped herself up on one leg and skipped along very quickly indeed. Her progress wasn't aided by the three dogs, Strudel the retriever, Nanook the enormous black Newfoundland and Taxi, the skinny black and white cattle dog. The dogs all darted constantly around Hester's ankles, getting underfoot and almost tripping her up as she hopped from one room to the next.

"…and this is the ballroom, and the servants quarters – not that we have any servants!"

"What about Aidan?" Issie said.

"Oh, he's got his own place down the hill, next to the stables. Farm manager's cottage – very sweet. Right next to the duck pond," Hester said. "I'll show you when we do our outdoor tour. Now follow me up the stairs."

The grand, wooden staircase stood proudly at the centre of the manor. "There are seven bedrooms upstairs," Aunt Hester explained as she reached the top of the landing. "This one is your room."

Hester swung open the door and beckoned for

Issie to step inside. The room was enormous, but it felt cosy. The walls were papered with the most beautiful wallpaper Issie had ever seen, illustrated with old-fashioned drawings of exquisite Thoroughbreds standing with their jockeys dressed up in racing silks. Above the grand fireplace was a large oil painting of a beautiful grey horse with a long, silky mane. The horse was captured in action, cantering with his neck arched, and his proud head held high.

"Isn't he beautiful?" Hester smiled. "That's Avignon. He was my very favourite horse – a Swedish Warmblood stallion. I just adored him! Oh, I could look at this painting for ever..." Her voice trailed off as she stared at the painting. Then she picked up Issie's luggage, throwing the bags on the four-poster bed.

"Come on," she smiled at Issie, "that's the tour over and done with. Let's get out of here and go and see that horse of yours, shall we?"

If Hester had bounded swiftly around the manor, the long walk down to the stables seemed to take the spring out of her step. The driveway wound along the side of the manor then down past the garden, bordered by a stand of enormous puriri trees. Beneath the trees were gardens filled with magnolias, camellias and ferns, bordering a green lawn covered in daisies. At the far end of the lawn was a tennis court which looked as if it had seen better days. There were weeds springing up everywhere and the dilapidated old tennis net sagged in the middle.

"As you can imagine, tennis is not my priority right now." Hester said, tapping her cast. "Still, if you want play, I'm sure I've got racquets somewhere."

They continued their walk to the stables. Hester had to pause for a rest several times on the way, propping herself up against the huge boulders that lined the driveway to catch her breath. The three dogs all lay down obediently at her side each time she stopped, waiting until she instructed them to move again.

"This is why I need your help, Isadora darling," Hester said. "I simply can't get about to manage the animals. And Aidan couldn't possibly do everything on his own. Besides, Butch cannot abide Aidan, so that would never do.

"Who's Butch?" Issie asked. Just as she said this, round the corner from behind the stables lumbered a massive, black, hairy boar.

"Butch!" Hester cried. "Come and meet Isadora!"

The pig grunted happily and broke into a jog as he came towards them. His tiny little trotters looked like they might not be able to support the enormous bulk of the beast for much longer as he wobbled along.

"Butch is one of my superstars," Hester cooed as she reached down to feed the pig a carrot and give him a vigorous scratch behind the ears with a stick. "Do you know he's been in three TV commercials already this year? He's the pig in that bank ad – you know, the one with the piggy banks? He's rather famous, aren't you, Butchy? Shall we show Isadora some of your tricks?"

Hester put down her scratching stick, stood up from the boulder and produced another carrot which she held high above her head. "Beg, Butch!" she commanded. The pig grunted and then shifted his enormous weight, slumping back to sit on his haunches. Slowly he adjusted his position and lifted one front trotter and then the other off the ground so that he was balanced back on his hind legs. He looked just like a begging dog.

"Good lad!" Hester praised him and tossed the carrot up in the air. Butch opened his mouth and snapped at the carrot as it fell, crunching it up eagerly in his vast jaws.

Hester produced a second carrot. This time she held it directly in front of her like a magician brandishing a wand. "Play dead!" she commanded the pig. Butch gave a grunt and then fell dramatically, landing on the ground with a leaden thud. He lay perfectly still, even when Hester gave him a gentle prod with her foot. "Nice and dead," she cooed. "What a good pig! Now, Butch, up!" Butch grunted again and lifted his head, then braced himself with his front trotters and rather ungracefully pushed himself up again so that he was standing facing Aunt Hester.

"Well done, good Butch," she said as she fed him one more carrot.

"How did you teach him the tricks?" Issie asked.

"Oh, pigs are very easy to train; they're smarter than dogs," Hester said. "I've had Butch since he was a little piglet and I always knew he was clever. When he was a piglet Aidan caught him in the veggie garden and pelted him with an acorn. Butch has never forgiven him. That's why you'll have to look after him and keep his training up while you're here."

"But I don't know anything about pig training!" Issie spluttered.

"Don't worry, I'll explain everything. It's all quite simple," Hester said. "I've figured out a roster. Aidan will take care of the chickens and ducks. They've got a big role in this movie and they all need to learn their cues. One of the ducks needs to open a door – you can

44

imagine the fuss he's made learning that... You're in charge of the rabbits," Hester continued. "There are seven of them and they're quite a funny bunch, I can tell you. You'll look after Butch too, of course, and then there's Meadow and Blossom."

"More pigs?" Issie asked.

"No, dear, a calf and a goat. Both of them are frightfully naughty and I'm afraid I've fallen quite behind in their training. You'll have to be rather firm with them."

"What exactly am I going to teach them?" Issie asked, feeling nervous.

"Oh, the usual. When to stop and go, nodding and shaking their heads... all the standard stuff," Hester said. "It's such bad timing to break my leg just when all my little stars are needed for such a big movie. *Tenderfoot Farm,* that's what it's called. It's an American crew. They're coming here next month to start filming. They need barnyard animals that can act on cue – and that's where I come in. My darlings are the best in the business." Hester gave Butch one last scratch behind the ears with the stick and then began to walk again towards the stables. The pig now joined them, trotting alongside with the dogs.

"The horses are my first love, of course," Hester

said as they approached the stables. "Other animals are lovely, but there is something truly magical about horses, don't you think?" She gave Issie a strange look as she said this and Issie didn't know what to say. Even Aunty Hess would be shocked if she knew about Mystic.

Issie's grey gelding had been such a special horse. She had loved him so deeply; it felt like her world had been torn apart the day he died. But since then, well, maybe *magical* was exactly the word for it. Issie had missed her horse so much that at first she couldn't believe it when Mystic had come back to her. He would appear just when she needed him most – and not like some ghost or anything, but a real horse. He had saved Issie and Blaze on more than one occasion. If anyone believed in the magic that horses held within them, it was Issie. But Issie knew somehow instinctively that Mystic was her secret now – and anyway, how could she possibly explain it all to Aunt Hester?

The stable was a large building, just a single storey with wide weatherboard planks painted a clean, crisp apple-white. Next to the stable block was a covered arena, not like a dressage arena, but a round pen with high walls and tiered seating. "That's where I do all of my stunt training." Hester gestured to it as she breezed past the pen towards the enormous sliding barn doors that led into the stable complex.

"It's so beautiful in here!" Issie was amazed. The stable doors were pale, honey-coloured wood. Each stall had a horse's head carved ornately on the door and a horse's nameplate hanging from a hook.

"We have seven horses of our own here so there is plenty of room for Blaze," Hester said as they walked. "We've put her right here, in the nearest stall to your right. Why don't we check on her first and then you can meet the others?"

Issie walked up to the stall. She ran her hand over the carved head on the door. There was no nameplate on the hook, but she could hear her horse nickering softly on the other side of the door.

"Blaze? Hey, girl, it's me." Issie said.

The mare went quiet for a moment, listening to Issie's voice. Then she nickered back, louder this time. Issie could hear her shifting about anxiously in the stall. She opened the top half of the Dutch door and bolted it back. There was Blaze, standing in the far corner of the stall next to her hay net. She nickered happily and came over immediately to Issie, nuzzling her soft muzzle against Issie's hands, taking a carrot from her palm. Issie raised her hand up and stroked just behind Blaze's ears, her fingers tangling in the mare's long flaxen mane.

"Well, isn't she something!" Aunt Hester said. "Your mother told me the whole story," she added, "so I knew your Blaze would be a beauty. But she's more than that, isn't she? She's a very special horse indeed."

Issie nodded silently.

"I know a thing or two about special horses myself," Hester said. "Come on. I want you to meet them." Hester walked over to the next stall and unbolted the door. "Come and say hello to Titan," she said.

Issie walked over and looked into the stall. It was completely empty. "Umm, Aunty Hess? There's no horse in here." Issie was confused. She stared at the unoccupied stall and back at her aunt, who had an amused smile on her face. And then she heard a noise, just a faint sound, the sound of a pony's hooves on the straw. Issie stuck her head right over the top of the Dutch door and there, hidden from view on the other side, was the smallest pony she had ever seen!

"Titan is a Falabella – a miniature horse," her Aunt said. "Nine hands tall. But such a big little horse, so much character! And quite the bossy-boots too! She keeps the big horses in line, I can tell you. Don't you, Titan?"

The tiny pony looked up at Issie and Hester. Her eyes were barely visible beneath her shaggy brown mane as she gratefully accepted Hester's offer of a carrot.

Hester left the top half of the Dutch door open and moved on to the next stall. "This is Dolomite," she said. Issie looked down, expecting to meet another miniature, but in fact Dolomite was just the reverse; he was an enormous bay Clydesdale with a broad white stripe running down his nose.

"Dolly is eighteen hands," Hester said. "You'd need a step ladder to get up on him, wouldn't you?"

Issie reached her hand up to pat Dolomite's nose. The gelding was so huge she had to stretch to reach him.

"He's a big softie. And very good for vaulting tricks," Hester said as she bustled along to the next stall.

"This is Diablo, the silly boy that broke my ankle," she said merrily. Diablo, a very handsome black and white piebald Quarter Horse, stuck his two-toned face over the stall. "Diablo loves doing cowboy tricks. He's a bit of show-off but I do love him," Hester said. "Diablo! Count to ten!" Hester barked at the horse.

The handsome piebald began to tap against the floor of the stall with his hoof, "one… two… three… four… five… six… seven… eight… nine… ten!"

Issie was amazed, but Aunt Hester just shrugged. "It's not so clever. A simple trick. I'll show you how it's done."

She moved across now to the other side of the stable and worked her way along the row, opening the doors to another two stalls. To Issie's surprise, each stall contained a palomino. The horses were so alike they were almost identical. "Meet the girls," Hester said. "That's Paris Hilton and this one is Nicole Ritchie." Hester stood there in front of the golden mares. "They're as pretty as their namesakes but much smarter." She grinned.

Hester opened the doors to the last two stalls now. "This is Scott," she said, patting the nose of a large skewbald gelding with a white face. "He's not the star, you understand, hasn't got that look-at-me quality in front of the cameras. But he's a good solid bet as a horse to play supporting roles."

Issie fed Scott a carrot while Hester walked on to the last stall and gave a soft cluck. In the final stall was a handsome bay gelding. "Tornado is the bad boy of the stable," Hester sighed. "But he will do absolutely anything you ask if you bribe him with peppermints. He used to be my eventing mount years ago. I still hunt on him occasionally. At least I did until this season."

She tapped her plaster cast and shrugged. "I have tried to teach Tornado tricks like the others but frankly he doesn't want to know! He's very bright; I guess he thinks it's beneath him." She pulled a mint from her pocket and slipped it to the bay horse, who snuffled it down happily and poked his head over the stall looking for more.

"Well!" Hester put her arm around her niece's shoulder and gave Issie a squeeze as she looked about contentedly. "Now you've met just about everyone. What do you think?"

Issie gave her aunt a hug back. "I think this place is totally mad!" She grinned. "And I think this could be my best holiday ever!"

CHAPTER 4

Issie could feel the waves lapping at her feet. Her toes wriggled in the delicious warm sea. Suddenly a sharp nip on her big toe woke her up and she sat bolt upright in bed. Her feet, which were sticking out from under the duvet, were being vigorously licked by Strudel the golden retriever.

"Ewww! Gross! Strudel, get out!" Issie shrieked, throwing a pillow at the dog, who loped happily off through the door.

Issie jumped out of bed and picked the pillow up off the floor. The alarm clock said it was only six a.m. Bleary-eyed, she changed into her jeans and a navy v-neck jersey before heading downstairs. She wasn't getting caught by Aidan in her pink pussycat pyjamas in the kitchen a second time.

"Ah-ha! I sent Strudel up to wake you. I see she did her job nicely." Aunt Hester smiled as Issie walked into the kitchen. "Did you sleep well?"

"Uh-huh," Issie replied.

"Sit down. I've made us some breakfast," Hester said. She began to dish up some rather strange-looking lumpy objects out of a frying pan.

"Pancakes!" Hester said brightly. Then she frowned and looked at them again, "Or are they griddle scones? I can't quite remember what I put in the recipe and I got confused halfway through... anyway, here's some maple syrup, If you pour enough of this on them I'm sure they'll taste fine!"

Issie ate a mouthful of pancake and discovered that they tasted just as odd as they looked.

"Now," Hester said as she watched her niece slowly eating, "the weather promises to be just beautiful today. Why don't you take Blaze and go explore the farm? It goes for miles, you know. I was just about to find you a map and then I got sidetracked with the pancakes..." Aunt Hester put down the pan and began rummaging through the kitchen draws. She pulled out a piece of dog-eared paper. "Here we are – a map of Blackthorn Farm." Hester spread the pale parchment out on the kitchen table.

"Our land stretches from Blackthorn Forest here at the rear of the property," her finger traced along the dotted red line, "all the way to the east along the edge of the forest to Lake Deepwater, and then up along the ridge of the hills to the Coast Road until you reach the sea."

Issie looked at the map and hesitated for a moment. "But Aunty Hess, shouldn't I be helping Aidan with the animals?"

"Oh, there's plenty of time for that!" Hester smiled. "Aidan will manage for now, I'm sure. You need to get your bearings first before you start work. It's such a lovely day; it doesn't do horses or girls any good to be cooped up inside."

The dogs bounded along beside Issie as she walked down the limestone driveway and through the heavy wooden stable doors.

"It's me, girl!" Issie called to her horse as she hurriedly unbolted the top half of the Dutch door. Blaze immediately thrust her head over the door, nuzzling Issie and nickering happily.

"Hey, Blaze," Issie said, "did you miss me? Were you

lonely here all by yourself in the stable?" She fed the mare a carrot and felt the tickle of her velvet muzzle on her fingers. "C'mon, we're going for a ride."

As Issie led Blaze through the stable block towards the back door the other horses nickered out friendly greetings to her. Diablo put his pretty black and white patchy head over the top of his stable door and gave her a vigorous whinny.

"Good morning to you too, Diablo!" Issie grinned. Blaze skipped along lightly at Issie's side, her hooves chiming out a delicate trip-trap against the concrete floor of the stables.

Issie led Blaze through the cattle pens at the rear of the stables and used the fence rails to mount up. Then she pulled the map out of the pocket of her shirt. To her right was the duck pond and a small cottage surrounded by magnolia trees, which Issie figured must be Aidan's house. To the left was a five-bar wooden gate and on the other side of the gate was a dirt track, bordered on the far side by dense forest. Issie looked at the map. There was a gate and then a red dotted boundary line marked: CATTLE TRACK.

"This must be it, Blaze," Issie said to her horse. "According to the map, this track takes us all the way along the edge of the forest and then down through the farm to Lake Deepwater."

Issie clucked Blaze through the gate, doing the latch back up after herself. Ahead of her the red clay path ran all the way along the ridge next to the trees.

Blaze jogged nervously along the track, her ears pricked forward, nostrils flared. The mare was keyed up after spending the day in the truck and then being kept stabled last night. All she wanted to do was run.

"Easy, Blaze, easy," Issie steadied the mare, keeping a firm grip on the reins. She knew she shouldn't give Blaze her head so soon, especially in a new environment. Then again, Issie had been cooped up too and she couldn't bear the thought of a quiet walk any more than her horse could.

"OK, OK, you win." Issie smiled. She readied herself, standing up in her stirrups in two-point position, and slackened her grip on Blaze's reins.

Issie felt her stomach lurch suddenly as Blaze lunged forward and she got left behind. She quickly regained her balance and crouched low over Blaze's neck as the mare stretched out into a gallop. The red clay soil was hard from the summer sun and Blaze's hooves beat out a clean rhythm as she ran. Issie sat very still, barely moving in the saddle. She didn't need to urge her forward, Blaze was running for the love of it.

To the right of the ridge track the land dropped dramatically away down a steep grassy slope which was dotted with surefooted, grazing sheep. To the left was the forest, a dense blur of trees and shadows flashing black and green as they galloped past.

Suddenly Blaze let out a snort and swerved hard, away from the trees. Issie shrieked as she felt the pony's centre of gravity shift out from beneath her. For a moment Blaze teetered sickeningly close to the edge of the track and Issie was terrified that they would plunge down the slopes of the steep bank.

"No!" Issie shouted, thinking fast and pushing Blaze back on to the track with her legs, yanking at the mare's mouth with the left rein. Blaze responded instantly, correcting herself, and Issie regained her seat and gathered up the reins again.

Why had Blaze spooked like that? Maybe Issie had been wrong to let her gallop too soon. She had just decided it would be best to pull the mare up and trot for the rest of the track, when she heard a noise in the forest that changed her mind.

From the dark blur of the trees right beside them

came the sound of an animal crashing through the undergrowth. Even though Blaze was in full gallop the creature was keeping pace with them. It was now so close it was running alongside them. Issie felt a chill of horror. Whatever it was, it was big. And it was after them.

Now Issie understood why Blaze had bolted. She wasn't misbehaving after all. She was terrified!

Issie tried to look into the woods to see what was chasing them, but Blaze was moving so quickly and the woods were so thick and impenetrable, it was impossible. She couldn't see a thing. One thing was certain: she wasn't waiting around to see what it was!

"C'mon, girl," Issie clucked the mare on now, asking her for more speed. Blaze immediately responded, her stride lengthening, her neck stretched out. Issie felt the pony surge forward underneath her and she bent down low over her mane. The wind whipped against her face, stinging her eyes and whistling around her ears. She strained to listen, trying to hear if the creature was still following them, but any sound was drowned out by the blur of Blaze's speed.

It was only when they had reached the ridge of the hill that Issie sensed she and Blaze were alone once more. Whatever was in the woods, they had outrun it.

"Easy, girl, steady. It's OK." Issie pulled the mare

back. Blaze's flanks were heaving, and her neck was wet and frothy with sweat. "It's all right, girl. I don't know what that was, but it's gone now," Issie said, giving Blaze a comforting pat on the neck. She knew that she was trying to reassure herself as much as her horse. She listened, but there was still no sound of anything following them. Issie turned her head slowly and looked back up the track behind her. There was nothing there.

Ahead of them, the red dirt path ran close to the forest for another mile or so, then the trail cut down through the paddocks towards the lake. *Good*, Issie thought, *the sooner we get away from the trees the better.* She coaxed Blaze into a trot. They needed to keep moving, keep up the pace until they were away from the trees.

When the track finally veered away from the forest and down into farmland again Issie heaved a sigh of relief and let Blaze walk for a while. She still couldn't believe it. What was that creature in the forest? It must have been almost as big as Blaze – and almost as fast. One thing was certain: she wasn't taking the same way home!

Issie took out her map again. Lake Deepwater was maybe an hour away. Once they reached the lake they could loop around on to the Coast Road and go back to the manor that way. Then they wouldn't have to ride back past the forest again.

Issie had the feeling they were still being followed. "Trust your horse, Issie," she reminded herself. Horses have strong instincts for danger and if Blaze was calm now, that meant they had nothing to fear. Besides, they were in open grassy pasture so if anything was following them Issie would be able to see it coming.

They had been riding on for about an hour when they reached the brow of a hill and looked down at Lake Deepwater. The lake, which was smaller than Issie had expected, sat in a natural basin. The area around the banks was grassy pasture, dotted with a few willow trees by the water's edge and on the far side next to the water there was a thick grove of blackthorn trees.

Issie looked at her map again. It looked like the Coast Road lay just over the ridge beyond those blackthorn trees. Once she was on the road it wouldn't take her long to get back to the farm again.

Issie was about to ride Blaze towards the trees when she heard a crashing noise from over the ridge that made her freeze. *Not again!* Issie thought.

She began to gather up Blaze's reins, looking around, trying to decide which way they should run. The noise was getting louder now. It sounded like thunder; Issie could feel the rumble shaking the ground beneath her.

With relief, she realised that this sound was nothing like the one coming from the trees earlier that morning. No, this was a sound she had heard many times before and it was unmistakeable. It was the sound of hoofbeats.

From behind the blackthorn trees the horses came into view. Issie watched in amazement as the herd rounded the edge of the lake at a gallop, bucking and swerving wildly as they ran. At the head of the herd was a thick-set buckskin with a bushy black mane and fiery eyes. The buckskin was followed by a stocky strawberry roan, a black and brown skewbald and a motley assortment of buckskins and bays. At the rear of the herd was a grey mare and a chestnut skewbald with a white face, both of them with foals running at their feet. The foals stuck close to their mother's side. The grey mare's foal was jet black. The skewbald's foal was the spitting image of its mother with chestnut and white patches all over its body and a broad blaze down its face.

The horses pulled up on the other side of the lake and stared at Issie and Blaze. They were stocky and broad, Issie noticed, and not really horses at all. Most of them were ponies, not much bigger than thirteen hands high.

Their manes and tails were ragged and sunbleached. Their coats were dusty and mud-caked. These were wild ponies, totally unbroken. Maybe they had never even seen a human before.

Blaze, who had been pacing nervously beneath Issie this whole time, suddenly let out a shrill whinny. To Issie's surprise the mare's call was immediately returned as a horse rose up before them over the brow of the hill.

This horse's whinny was brutal and fierce. It sounded to Issie like a battle cry. There was something defiant and challenging about the call and Issie realised what it was. It was the cry of a stallion.

The stallion who stood on the ridge was nothing like the rest of the herd. Those wild ponies were no bigger than Blaze. The stallion, on the other hand, was huge. He must have been at least sixteen hands high and his coat, which was jet black, shone in the sun. He had no markings, except for a slender white stripe which ran down his forehead.

The black horse held himself so proudly with his neck arched and his tail held erect. He had the noble bearing that comes with fine breeding – his face handsome and aquiline, his body large and powerful. It was as if he was sculpted from granite. Issie was possessed with the feeling she had seen this horse somewhere before.

But where? Then she realised. He looked just like the painting on her bedroom wall, the portrait of Avignon, Aunt Hester's great grey stallion.

For a moment the stallion and Issie stood staring directly at each other. Then the big, black horse gave an arrogant snort and began to canter down the hill after his herd, rounding on his mares and threatening them back into formation with his ears flat back. With his teeth bared and his magnificent neck arched, the stallion nipped and squealed at his mares as he cantered. The grumpy buckskin mare nipped defiantly back at him, but even she obeyed eventually, and within a few minutes the stallion had gathered the whole herd together and was standing between Issie and his mares.

With the herd corralled safely behind him, the stallion seemed uncertain what to do next. He cantered back and forth and then stopped, pawing the ground restlessly as if he was considering his next move. Then he raised his head and let out a war cry that was filled with fury, like the bellow of a wild boar.

Issie's face went pale with fear. Beneath her she felt Blaze stiffen in terror.

I'm so stupid, Issie thought, furious with herself. *He's a stallion and we're a threat to his herd and now he's going to attack. We should have run the moment I saw him. Why didn't we run?*

The black stallion was close now – too close for Issie and Blaze to turn and run. His eyes were black with anger. His teeth were bared, ready to fight.

Issie tried to steady Blaze, but the chesnut mare trembled with fear and rage. What would Blaze do if the black horse attacked? She was no match for a stallion! No. They had to make a run for it. What else could they do? After all, there was no one here to save them.

And then Issie realised. Mystic! The little grey gelding always seemed to know when they needed help. Well, she was certainly in trouble right now. Surely Mystic would appear? Issie's eyes scanned the crest of the hill. Nothing. Maybe she should call for him?

"Mystic!" Issie yelled. Her voice came out reedy and shrill, strangled by her fear.

Mystic had died trying to save Issie. Since then he had saved Issie and Blaze so many times. He was always there when she really needed him. So where was her grey pony now?

The shrill whinny of a horse shook Issie back to reality. Not Mystic's whinny, but the piercing call of the stallion. In that split second Issie made up her mind.

She couldn't do nothing and rely on Mystic to come and fight her battles; there wasn't time for that. She would have to find her own way out of this.

OK, so they needed to run – but where? Issie looked around for a way to escape. To her left were the grassy slopes of the hill. Should she try to outrun the black horse? Could they make it up the hill? She looked now to the right of her at the still, deep waters of the lake. *No way out*, Issie thought. *What now?*

As the black horse began to gallop towards them Issie felt her pulse race and she realised she knew what to do. They weren't going to run away from this horse. They were going to run straight for him.

"C'mon, girl!" Issie said to her pony. And with an almighty kick she drove Blaze on straight at the stallion in a hard gallop. Blaze was only too willing. The mare's eyes were fixed on the black stallion. She was ready to fight.

Issie held her path as the two horses bore down on each other. *Keep your head,* she told herself, *keep going. Just a bit closer...*

Suddenly, just as the horses were moments away from colliding, Issie hauled desperately on Blaze's right rein. "Go, Blaze!" Issie yelled at her horse. Shocked, the mare leapt forward at Issie's command, up into the air and down again into the murky waters of the lake.

There was an awful moment when Blaze hit the water, lost her footing and stumbled forward. Issie managed to pull the mare's nose up and ride her on, keeping her at a canter as she regained her feet. Then they ploughed on through the mud and the reeds, the water splashing up Issie's jodhpurs, seeping into the leather of her boots. Blaze snorted in fear as she cantered in deeper; the water was up to her chest now. Issie looked back over her shoulder. The stallion was behind them. He had followed them into the lake, but he was hesitating. Instead of cantering after them he was weaving backwards and forwards, as if uncertain whether to go any deeper into the water.

"Come on, girl!" Issie gave Blaze a sharp kick in the ribs. "Come on, girl! Let's go!" The kick made Blaze leap forward again. Issie looked around her and realised that they were already in the middle of the lake. Then they were past the middle and heading back out the other side – and the water hadn't so much as gone over Issie's boots!

So much for Lake Deepwater, she thought with relief. *More like Lake Shallowmud.*

Issie looked back again over her shoulder. The stallion had given up on them and turned around now, trotting out of the lake and back towards his herd.

"We've lost him, Blaze! Not much further to go, girl!" Issie gave her mare a slappy pat on her neck. Once they reached the other side, Issie was pretty sure that just over the ridge they'd find the Coast Road that would lead them home to Blackthorn Manor.

"Good girl, Blaze!" Issie gave the mare another big pat on her neck as Blaze leapt up the muddy slopes of the bank and on to the green grass that bordered the lake.

She had been worried that Blaze might have been exhausted from the chase that morning, but the mare still seemed to have plenty of speed left in her. As they rode up the grassy slope and hit the dirt track that led them along the Coast Road back to the farm, Blaze stretched out at full gallop.

The black horse hadn't followed them. They were safe. All the same, Issie stayed low over Blaze's neck and let her run. She didn't stop galloping until they were another two miles down the road. And she didn't stop checking over her shoulder until they were safely home at Blackthorn Manor.

CHAPTER 5

Aunt Hester sat on the front veranda of Blackthorn Manor with a mug of piping hot tea and a copy of the *Times*. As Issie and Blaze trotted down the long, leafy avenue of the limestone driveway towards her she looked up and gave them a cheery wave. Then suddenly she stopped waving. Her face turned dark with concern and she propped herself up with her walking stick and hobbled down the steps that led from the veranda and across the cherry-tree lawn to meet the horse and rider.

"What on earth happened to you two?" Hester said as she took Blaze's reins. Issie dismounted and promptly flopped down, lying spread-eagled on the cool, green lawn next to her horse. She was completely exhausted. Blaze, who was caked with dried sweat and mud from her marathon galloping efforts, looked even more wretched than her rider.

"We got into a bit of trouble – well, two bits of trouble actually," Issie said.

"I can see that!" Aunt Hester said. "Isadora, how did you end up in this state? Are you all right?"

"I'm fine, Aunty Hess. Honest. I just need a minute to get back up..." Issie took a deep breath and forced herself to stand up again, reaching out to take Blaze's reins. Aunt Hester reluctantly handed them to her.

"Her stable is all ready for her. Aidan mucked it out this morning. I'll come with you and help you untack. And on the way you're going to tell me what in the blazes you two have been getting up to out there!"

As they walked slowly down the driveway to the stables Issie told her aunt about the animal in the woods that had stalked them along the ridge track.

"So you didn't see this creature at all?" Hester asked. "Not even a glimpse?"

"It was too dark in the trees and we were moving so fast that I couldn't see," Issie said. "All I know is that it was big. Really big. It could keep up with Blaze even when she was galloping."

"Could it have been one of the dogs? Did they follow you out?" Aunt Hester asked.

"It was far too big to be Taxi or Strudel," Issie said, "but I suppose it could have been Nanook." The enormous black Newfoundland was large enough to have made the crashing noises she had heard.

"Oh, I doubt it. Nanook never goes for a walk without me. She's bone idle and as slow as a wet week." Hester dismissed the idea. Then she paused for a moment. "Could it, well, could it have been a cat?"

Issie looked at her aunt. "What do you mean?"

"Oh, I don't mean like a common moggy, dear," Aunt Hester said. "No. I mean a big cat, a mountain cat. There's a myth in these parts, you know, about a black cat that lives wild in the hills. They say it escaped from a zoo, and I suppose it's possible since there was once a wildlife park not far from here. They had antelope and lions and all sorts. When the wildlife park closed down all the animals were shipped off, but this particular black cat escaped and they never found it again. I've always thought the whole story sounded rather ridiculous. You hear a lot of tall tales about that sort of thing when you live out this way. Still, people do believe the myth. The Grimalkin they call him. The witch's cat.

Although I can't imagine that even a witch would be too pleased if she came across an enormous great panther! Old Bill Stokes who lives down on the Coast Road farm claims he saw it one night. He said a great black cat the size of a bear came out of the undergrowth and attacked one of his sheep, dragged it off right in front of his eyes. Of course they never found any sign of the sheep – and old Bill Stokes does like a drink so his accounts cannot always be relied upon..."

"Well, whatever it was, Blaze was terrified of it," Issie said.

"I haven't heard any reports of lost stock or anything unusual lately," Hester mused. "I think the best thing we can do is to let Cameron know about it. He's the local ranger with the Blackthorn Hills Conservation Trust. He's coming out to see me tomorrow and this is exactly the sort of thing he deals with. If there's a wild beastie in the woods he'll soon see to it."

"Do you think he'll believe me?" Issie said.

"Why?" her Aunt said briskly. "Do you often go making up stories about being stalked by phantom creatures and coming home covered in mud? Of course he'll believe you! He's a good man, Cameron. If there's something out there he'll find it."

They had reached the stables now and Issie undid the girth and slipped off Blaze's saddle while Aunt Hester hobbled across the stable to fetch the mare some hard feed. Issie took Blaze out to the rear of the stables and hosed her down in the wash bay to get rid of the sweat and dirt, using a sweat scraper to dry the mare off before letting her loose in the stall. Hester gave Blaze the tub full of chaff and pony nuts and they stood there together watching as she ate.

"Now," Hester said, "you said you had two bits of trouble? What else did you find out there?" Issie told her about the herd of horses she had seen down at Lake Deepwater.

"Now this is a mystery that I can solve," Hester said brightly. "Those are Blackthorn Ponies you're talking about. I'm surprised you've never heard of them before."

"Blackthorn Ponies?" Issie said.

"A breed unique to this area. There's been a herd roaming the high country here for over twenty years," Hester said. "They're wild horses, descendants of a few local riding ponies that got loose and then refused to be caught again. The herd has survived somehow over the years; they are very hardy little specimens I must say. There must be at least twenty of them by now?"

"Closer to thirty, I think," Issie said. "Aunty Hess, there was a stallion with them. He was at least sixteen hands, much taller than the rest of them, and jet black."

"Really?" Hester looked interested at this. "No, I don't recall a stallion, but then I haven't seen the herd in quite some time."

"It was the stallion that attacked us – me and Blaze," Issie continued. "It was my fault. He was so beautiful and I was so busy watching him, I didn't think. Then when I realised we were in danger and we needed to run it was too late. He was going crazy trying to protect his herd. We had to swim the lake to get away."

"Ah, so that's where all the mud has come from!" Hester nodded. "Well, you were lucky, my dear. A stallion can be as ferocious as a tiger when he thinks he's protecting his herd. If it actually was his herd. You say this horse didn't look like the others?"

"Well, there were two foals – the black one looked just like him. But none of the others… There was something about him, Aunty Hess. He was so handsome, he reminded me of that painting on my bedroom wall."

Aunt Hester raised an eyebrow at this. "Avignon? He reminded you of my darling Avignon? Well, I suppose anything is possible. Avignon was a great jumper, you know. Fences could never hold him and he frequently made his escape into the hills. I suppose on one of his great adventures he might have found the wild herd and bred with one of the Blackthorn mares." Hester smiled. "Wouldn't that be a treat? If my great grey stallion had sired a son – and a few grandsons by the sound of it – and now they're running about the countryside following in his footsteps. You say the little black foal looked just like him?"

"Uh-huh." Issie nodded.

"Well, this is very exciting news!" Aunt Hester said. Her smile suddenly faded. "Oh no. I've left lunch in the oven! It will be burnt to a crisp by now – if it hasn't set fire to the kitchen!" She turned towards the stable door and began to hop off briskly with her walking stick.

"Aunty Hess, don't be ridiculous. You can't run in a plaster cast. I'll dash back and turn off the oven," Issie said.

"If it's burnt on the outside don't throw it away. Just cut the black bits off. That's what I usually do," Aunt Hester called after her as Issie ran out of the stable doors.

When she arrived at the house Issie found what looked like the remains of a cottage pie burnt to a crisp on the top and promptly put it in the pig's bin before Aunt Hester could try to salvage it.

Issie stood there for a moment and stared at the charred remains on top of the bucket of pig slops. *Another narrow escape in my first day at Blackthorn Farm.* She smiled to herself. Avoiding Aunt Hester's cooking efforts was one thing, but wild stallions and black panthers were another matter entirely. Issie knew they had been lucky to escape with their lives today.

When Issie checked in on her horse at the stables later that afternoon Blaze seemed none the worse for wear after her adventures. She fed Blaze her chaff and pony nuts for dinner and hung up a hay net for the mare to munch through overnight. Then she checked on the other horses in their stalls.

Issie was adjusting Diablo's stable rug when she heard a noise behind her. "Miaow!" The sound made her jump and she turned around to see Aidan leaning over the stable door, smiling at her.

"Ohmygod, Aidan! You scared me!"

Aidan pushed his long dark hair back out of his eyes. "It wasn't me – it was the Grimalkin, the witch's cat of Blackthorn Ridge!" He grinned at her.

Issie threw a sponge out of Diablo's grooming kit at the stall door and Aidan ducked as it flew past his ear.

"I'm not imagining it, Aidan. I was chased by something today in the woods. I'm not saying it was some imaginary cat. I don't know what it was, but it followed me and Blaze and it was fast and it was huge." Issie stood her ground.

"Hey," Aidan raised both his palms up as if surrendering the conversation to her, "I believe you. There's a big kitty out there who wants a saucer of milk and a pony."

"Aidan!"

"No, seriously, Issie, I do believe you. The horses have all been very spooky lately and last week we lost two chickens from the henhouse. I thought it was probably a stoat, but maybe it was whatever was chasing you and Blaze." Aidan cast his eyes over Diablo. The piebald was shifting restlessly in his stall. "Horses can sense things, you know," Aidan said quietly. "They know when there's trouble about."

"So can pigs," Issie added.

"What?" Aidan said.

"Well, I hear that Butch doesn't like you much, so I guess he knows trouble when he sees it too." Issie grinned.

"Yes," said Aidan, "yes, I guess he does."

After she'd helped Aidan feed all the horses and lock

the stalls for the night, Issie took the leftover scraps of burnt lunch, potato peelings and last night's supper and went to visit Butch.

"Don't worry, Butch, it's just me. Aidan isn't here," she reassured the big, black pig. Then she tipped the scraps into his trough and, while he ate, gave him a firm scratch behind the ears with his favourite scratching stick.

Once Butch was fed she headed down past the stables to the cattle pens where Blossom and Meadow were kept. Blossom looked at Issie gratefully with her scary yellow goat eyes as she filled the feed bin with carrots and apple slices.

Issie pulled a carrot out of her pocket. "Count to five, Blossom!" Issie instructed, holding the carrot over the goat's head just as Aunt Hester had done with Butch the other day. "Count, Blossom!" Issie commanded again.

Blossom looked up, snatched the carrot out of Issie's hand and then carried on eating.

"Ummm, well, I guess I'll start training you properly tomorrow," Issie said.

In the pen next to Blossom, Meadow, a patchy chestnut and white Hereford calf, was pacing up and down waiting for her supper. She gave Issie a friendly lick with her coarse sandpaper tongue as she entered her pen. Issie had heated a bottle full of milk for the young calf and, as she produced the teat, Meadow suctioned on immediately and began to drink, pushing and nudging at Issie as the bottle began to empty.

"Wow! You have a big appetite for a little cow," Issie said. Meadow had emptied the bottle now and was sucking on Issie's fingers instead. "Stop it!" she giggled, edging backwards out of Meadow's pen and locking the gate after herself.

Before she left the stables Issie stopped in once more at Blaze's stall to say goodnight. "Sleep tight, Blaze," she said, patting the mare's velvet-soft nose. Blaze nickered softly in return and Issie gave her one last carrot before she locked the stall doors behind her.

The first day at Blackthorn Farm had given Issie more than enough news to tell her friends. Luckily Aunt Hester did have the Internet so she didn't need to use carrier pigeons after all. "But what an excellent idea!" Hester had laughed when Issie suggested this as a joke. "Carrier pigeons! I shall have to train some up just in case. We are always having problems with the phone lines here after the autumn storms. A pigeon might come in handy!"

Issie wasn't sure if her aunt was joking or not. **After all**, she told Stella in her email, **this is a place where it is considered perfectly normal for ducks to open doors, and tomorrow I'm supposed to be teaching the goat how to bow. Aunt Hester says it's time I filled her shoes and began animal training. Yikes! It's like I'm Dr Doolittle or something. I can't believe I am missing the summer dressage series. Say hi to Coco and to Kate and Toby. Miss you. BFF XXX Issie.**

Issie only had to wait a few minutes after she'd sent her email before she heard the ping of an email coming back in return.

You think you've got it tough? Stella wrote back. **I wish I was teaching goats to bark or whatever you're doing. Meanwhile, I'm stuck here doing the summer dressage series and guess who is winning by, like, a million-kazillion points with her new pony and won't let any of us forget it? I'll give you a clue and that clue is STUCK-UP TUCKER! Oh I wish I was at the farm instead with all**

those animals - it sounds cool. Apart from
the bit where you got chased by the thing
in the forest and nearly killed by the wild
stallion. You're lucky that Blaze is so
fast - if it had been me on old slow-poke
Coco we'd have been eaten by the Grimalkin
already! BFF Stella XXX

Issie knew Stella didn't mean to make fun of her,
and neither did Aidan really. Still, she wished she had
never told anyone about the animal that had chased her
and Blaze on the ridge that morning. Now that Issie
was safely tucked up in bed at Blackthorn Manor she
was beginning to wonder if there really *was* an animal
in the woods or if her mind had been playing tricks on
her. It was only natural that Blaze would be a bit spooky
in her new home. Perhaps the mare had shied at her
own shadow and then bolted? Maybe there wasn't any
animal chasing them. After all, Issie hadn't actually seen
anything, had she?

No, she thought. *I didn't see anything – but I did hear
something.*

Blaze had heard it too. The mare hadn't just been
spooked – she had been terrified. She wasn't imagining
things. Something was out there; she was sure of it.

Issie fell asleep in her four-poster bed that night thinking about the creature in the woods. The moon was full in the sky outside and she could see the inky crest of the ridge outlined through her bedroom curtains as she dozed off.

When she woke again she guessed it must have been about midnight. The moon was still high in the sky, illuminating the view outside. Issie lay in bed and listened. In the hush of the night she could hear a scratching noise. It was coming from her door. She got up and quietly padded across the floor to open it, and there was Strudel, waiting patiently for her.

"Hello, Strudel. I suppose you want to come in?" Issie said.

The dog began to pad into the bedroom, but then suddenly she stopped. Her ears perked up and she froze. Then she turned tail and raced off again straight down the stairs. Issie grabbed her dressing gown and followed after her. A noise outside made the hairs on the back of her neck bristle as if someone had just walked over her grave. She could have sworn she had just heard the growl of a cat. A very big cat.

Outside on the back veranda Issie found Strudel standing alert. The dog was growling a low, rumbly growl.

"What is it, girl?" Issie said, putting her arm around the golden retriever. "Can you hear something?"

Suddenly a cacophony of squawking and flapping came from the henhouse. Strudel took off in the direction of the noise, her bark raising the alarm for the rest of the farm. Issie paused for a moment, peering blindly into the darkness and wondering what was out there waiting for her. Then she pulled on her boots and ran after Strudel down the driveway. Behind her she heard the barks of Taxi and Nanook, who had both heard Strudel's cry and were joining in the chase.

Down at the henhouse feathers were flying. The bantams were in a total state of terror, and Issie wished she had brought a torch with her so she could see what was going on. She opened the door to the henhouse and stepped inside, relying on the moonlight to guide her, trying to calm the frantic chickens so that she could check that they were all OK. She was just in the process of counting the chickens in the dark when she heard a squeal coming from the paddocks next to the stables. Strudel, Nanook and Taxi immediately bounded off in the direction of the sound, with Issie following.

The dog's cries were bloodcurdling and growing more frantic by the time Issie arrived at the stables.

She ran past the horses' stalls to the back door that led out to the duck pond and the cattle pens, pushing the enormous stable door open, and cast her eyes around the pens. The three dogs were barking wildly now.

"What is it, Strudel?" Issie asked. And then she saw the shape looming in front of her. Enormous and black, silhouetted against the night sky. The creature was sleek and huge – bigger than Nanook even – and it was moving fast, padding silently across the top of the fence-line, balanced on the wooden frame of the cattle pens.

The black shape of the Grimalkin disappeared into the darkness. The dogs were going crazy now, barking and wailing so loudly that Issie didn't hear the footsteps behind her. A hand on her shoulder made her jump.

"Shhh, it's me!" Aidan's voice calmed her down. "Just a second – let me find the torch – I've got one here somewhere…"

Aidan shone the torch beam on to the cattle pens. Issie peered at fence where she had seen the shadow of the Grimalkin just a moment before. There was nothing there now except the black night sky. Worried that Aidan would think she was silly, Issie couldn't decide whether to tell him that she'd seen the Grimalkin again. She didn't need to say anything, though, because Aidan spoke first.

"Go back to the house now, Issie," he said.

"Why, Aidan, what's wrong?" Issie moved closer.

"I said go back *now*!" Aidan shouted at her.

And then Issie saw why he was sending her away. The body of an animal lay covered in blood in the cattle pen at Aidan's feet. Issie rushed forward to help, and as she came closer she realised that it was Meadow. The chestnut and white calf was lying very still as Aidan bent down to examine her.

"Aidan! Ohmygod! I'll get the first-aid kit out of the tack room and…"

Aidan looked up at Issie. There were tears in his eyes. "It's no use," he said softly. "Issie, she's dead."

CHAPTER 6

Issie looked down at Meadow. The little calf's rust and white fur was smeared with blood and there were two deep gashes that looked like claw marks at her shoulder and throat. Aidan was right. There was no doubt that she was dead.

Aidan looked up at Issie. There were tears streaming down her face. "Honestly, Issie, I think she must have died instantly. Whatever did this was quick and deadly; she didn't suffer." He stood up and put his arm around Issie as she wiped the tears off her cheek with the sleeve of her pyjamas.

Aidan picked Meadow up and carried her inside the stables into one of the empty horse stalls, bolting the doors shut. Then he walked Issie back up the driveway to the manor, with the three dogs following noiselessly at their heels.

"What do you think it was, Aidan?" Issie asked.

"I don't know." Aidan shook his head. "Could have been the same thing that stalked you and Blaze."

"Poor Meadow," Issie said. "Can we give her a proper burial tomorrow under the magnolia trees?"

Aidan nodded. "Cameron will want to see her first. He'll need to figure out what it was that killed her. But yeah, of course we can."

As they reached the veranda, the lights came on inside the manor. "Aidan! Isadora! What's happening out here?" Aunt Hester emerged, wrapping her dressing gown around her.

"It's Meadow. She's been attacked," Aidan said. Hester turned quite pale.

"Is she all right?"

"She's dead," Aidan confirmed. "I've moved her into one of the stalls in the stables. I figured Cameron could check her over in the morning."

"Poor little meadow!" Hester shook her head.

"I saw it, Aunty Hess!" Issie said. "The Grimalkin. At least I think I did. It was on top of the cattle pens and then it was gone... If we'd only got there sooner..."

Hester put her arm around Issie. "Isadora, thank heavens you didn't get attacked by that thing. If you two and the dogs hadn't turned up and scared the Grimalkin off when you did, it may have hurt even more of the animals. Aidan, are all the animals safe for the night?"

"I've checked all the horses," Aidan told her. "They're all OK. I'm going to take one last check around the farm now and make sure everything is secure before I go back to bed. You two go inside and I'll see you both in the morning."

Hester nodded. "I'll report this to Cameron first thing. Come on, sweetie, it's two o'clock. Let's get you inside and back into bed. I'll make you a hot milk to help you sleep."

The hot milk did help. Issie didn't wake up again until nine a.m. When she finally came downstairs to breakfast Aidan was waiting for her at the kitchen table.

"How are you feeling?" he asked.

"Ummm, OK, I guess," Issie replied.

"I checked all the animals again this morning," Aidan said. "They're all fine. Whatever it was that killed Meadow is hopefully long gone…"

"If we'd only got there in time to save her..." Issie's voice was wobbly. She felt like she might cry and fought hard to hold back the tears.

"I still can't imagine what kind of animal would make those wounds." Aidan shook his head. "When Cameron arrives you can tell him what you saw and he can take a look at Meadow – maybe he'll have some ideas." Aidan picked up his riding gloves from the kitchen table and stood up.

"Meanwhile, we've got training to do." He smiled at her.

"We? You mean you and me?" Issie squeaked.

"Sure," Aidan said. "Didn't Hester tell you?" He looked at Issie's shocked face. "I guess she didn't. OK. Well, I'll head down to the stables and get the horses ready. You have some breakfast and then meet me at the round pen. We're doing some trick training."

"Really?" Issie felt a shiver of excitement run up her spine.

"See you there in fifteen!" Aidan said, already disappearing out the door, heading for the stables.

Issie felt almost too nervous to eat. Trick riding! It was just like in the movies. She managed to calm her butterflies enough to cram down a piece of toast and jam and then ran all the way down the driveway to the stable block where Aidan already had Diablo, Blaze and Paris saddled up and waiting at the side of the round pen.

"This is where we do most of the stunt training," Aidan explained. "I've been working on this stunt lately, I call it a 'Flying Angel'. I've been training Paris to do it with Diablo, and she's pretty good, but it's important that she can do the same trick with other horses and riders too. So I thought maybe today you could try it with her and Blaze?"

Issie nodded. "Umm, Aidan?" she asked.

"Yeah."

"What exactly is a 'Flying Angel'?"

Aidan grinned. "It's hard to explain. It's probably easier if you let me show you."

Aidan tied Blaze up outside the round pen and then he rode Diablo into the arena, leading Paris beside him. The wood-lined walls of the round pen were about two metres high and above them, circling the arena, were two rows of wooden bench seats. Issie climbed the stairs and sat down in a front row seat, watching silently as Aidan worked the horses in. He trotted back and forth in the middle of the arena on Diablo, keeping an eye on Paris, who was also wearing a saddle and bridle as she cantered riderless around the arena.

"Do you see how she's cantering in a circle like that?" Aidan called out to Issie. "She's been trained to do that. It makes it easier to do the trick if she's got a steady stride." As he said this he clucked Diablo forward and the black and white Quarter Horse began to canter behind the palomino.

Issie watched as Aidan cantered Diablo right up next to Paris so that he was riding neck and neck with the palomino mare. The two horses fell into step together, matching each other stride for stride.

Aidan smiled up at her. "Here we go!" he called out. And with that, he let go of Diablo's reins and sat bolt upright in the saddle with his arms spread out to either side for balance. Aidan rode one more lap around the round pen with his arms out. Issie could see him counting the beat in his head, figuring out his moment. Issie noticed that he was edging Diablo closer to Paris now, so that the piebald gelding was almost touching the palomino. Suddenly Aidan slipped his feet out of the stirrups and pivoted in the saddle, turning his body to face the wall. He cast one last look up at Issie, gave her a wave and then leapt.

Issie couldn't believe it! There was a split-second when Aidan was in midair that she imagined the worst.

He was going to fall and get trampled beneath Paris and Diablo's hooves. Then she saw Aidan grasp Paris' saddle with both hands and deftly swing his leg over the mare's back. Before she knew it, Aidan was in the saddle on Paris with the reins, which had been knotted around the palomino's neck, in his hands. By the time he rode around the arena to where Issie was seated he had a grin on his face and was waving to her as he went by.

Issie stood up, clapping wildly. "That was amazing!" she called out to him.

Aidan pulled Paris up in the centre of the arena and saluted to Issie, while Paris dropped to one knee underneath her rider, bowing theatrically.

"That," Aidan said, "is a Flying Angel."

He dismounted from Paris and walked over to Diablo, who was standing waiting for him. Then he led both horses up to the side of the arena and looked up at Issie. "Come on then – it's your turn. Why don't you bring Blaze into the arena and have a go?"

"But I don't know how…" Issie began.

"The only way to learn is to do it," Aidan said. "It's all about timing. You need to get Blaze into a rhythm next to Paris, then move them close, drop your stirrups and jump."

"You make it sound so simple," Issie said. She could

feel the butterflies in her tummy going berserk now.

"Yeah, well, it is simple once you've done it a few times. But the first time I made the jump was pretty hairy," Aidan admitted. "Are you ready to give it a go?"

Issie untied Blaze from the hitching post and led the mare in through the sliding wooden doors on to the sawdust floor of the round pen. As she put her foot in the stirrup, Blaze danced nervously.

"Easy, girl, it's OK," Issie cooed.

"I'm going up there to watch," Aidan said, gesturing to the stands above the arena. "Paris knows what to do – she'll just keep cantering around the arena. All you need to do is ride Blaze up next to her and make the jump." Issie nodded silently and as Aidan rode out on Diablo she turned Blaze around to face the palomino.

"Gee-up, Paris!" she called, waving her arms to get the mare moving on to the perimeter of the arena. Paris instantly reacted just as Aidan had said she would, high-stepping into a graceful canter, staying close to the wooden walls of the round pen.

As soon as Paris had cantered twice around the ring and settled into a steady stride, Issie clucked Blaze on and rode the liver chestnut mare out to join her. At first Blaze flinched a little as she edged closer to the palomino.

Then she seemed to understand what Issie wanted her to do and fell into a brisk canter next to Paris, running neck and neck alongside the pretty palomino.

"Steady, girl, that's it..." Issie said. She knotted Blaze's reins now, and then, very carefully, she let go. She was riding now without any hands, her arms floating up and up, helping her to balance so that eventually she was sitting straight up in the saddle with her arms spread out like angel wings.

"Now, turn your body to face Paris and drop your stirrups!" Aidan shouted at her from the side of the arena.

Issie looked up at him and gave him a quick nod. She did as he said, slipping her feet out of the stirrups so that she was now riding with the irons dangling at her feet. She turned her torso to face the wall and looked at the rise and fall of the palomino's empty saddle. She had to jump into that saddle. All she needed to do was reach out her hands and make that leap from Blaze's back on to Paris. Issie took a deep breath and counted down – ah-one, ah-two, ah—

She froze. She couldn't do this! It was crazy. She looked down and saw the horses' hooves churning beneath her on the sawdust floor of the arena. What if she fell? She would get trampled beneath Paris' hooves for sure!

"Come on, Issie! What are you waiting for?" Aidan called out. Issie felt her skin turning clammy, her tummy was churning with butterflies.

"Calm down," she told herself. "You can do this!"

She put her hands back out again and focused on getting back into position. Then she edged Blaze closer to Paris once more and waited until the two mares were matching each other stride for stride. Ah-one, ah-two, ah... noooo!

Issie pulled Blaze up to a halt. She could feel her heart beating like crazy, her palms were wet with sweat and she was trembling.

"Issie, Issie are you OK?" Aidan ran into the arena, his face grave with concern. "What happened? Why didn't you jump?"

Issie shook her head. "I don't know, Aidan. I thought I'd be able to do it but then I looked down and..."

"It's OK. Honest." Aidan smiled at her. "It's a pretty advanced stunt. It was probably too soon to ask you to try something like this. Don't worry about it. Really. We can try again some other time."

Aidan reached out to take Blaze's reins as Issie dismounted, but she was still holding them and instead of grasping the reins he found himself holding Issie's hand instead. There was a moment when Aidan and Issie were locked together, holding hands. Then the pair of them jumped back from each other and stood there looking embarrassed.

"Sorry, I mean, I didn't mean to…" Aidan stammered.

"No! I mean, that's fine…" Issie replied, looking at her feet. "I umm… I'd better put Blaze away now." She hurriedly led the chestnut mare out of the arena and back to the stable block, leaving Aidan standing there with Diablo and Paris.

"Ohmygod, could that have been any more embarrassing?" Issie murmured to Blaze, burying her head deep into her pony's mane as they stood together in Blaze's stall. Not only had she chickened out on doing the Flying Angel stunt, she had held hands with Aidan! This was just the worst!

Untacking Blaze quickly, Issie slipped out the back door of the stable, hoping she stood less chance of running into Aidan again if she went out that way. Then she ran across the lawn, up on to the porch and in through the back door of the manor.

As she walked towards the kitchen she thought for a moment that Aidan had somehow got back there before her. She could hear a man's voice in the kitchen talking with Aunt Hester. When she got nearer, though, she realised the voice didn't belong to Aidan.

"Isadora! Is that you? Come and meet Cameron," Aunt Hester said. "Cameron is the head ranger for the Blackthorn Hills Conservation Trust." Her Aunt smiled at the sandy-haired man in the khaki jacket sitting next to her at the table. "Cameron, I'd like you to meet Isadora, my favourite niece. She's the one who first sighted the Grimalkin up on Blackthorn Ridge yesterday."

"Is that so?" The ranger looked at Issie.

"Well, kind of..." Issie said. "Something was there and it chased me and my horse, but it was hidden by the trees so I never actually saw it. I just heard it."

The ranger cocked a suspicious eyebrow at this.

"But I did see it last night!" Issie added hastily. "It was right there on top of the cattle pens just before we found Meadow. It was balancing on the top of the wooden railings, running along them like a cat."

"Could it have been a cat?" Hester wondered.

"Ohmygod no! Not a normal cat. It was enormous. I mean, really huge," Issie said. "Bigger than Nanook even."

"Did you see what sort of an animal it was?" Cameron asked.

"Umm, not really. There was a full moon but it

was still very dark. It was black, I think, and it had a long thick tail, but I couldn't really see much more than that. It disappeared pretty fast and then Aidan found Meadow and..." Issie's voice trailed off as she remembered the awful events of the night before and the gruesome discovery of poor Meadow.

"Could have been a stray dog," the ranger assessed. "We've had a couple of reports of stock loss lately. Once a dog gets the taste for blood, they're trouble."

"It wasn't a dog," Issie said firmly.

The ranger looked at her again. "Well, whatever it was, we'll find it. I'm going to take a couple of men up to the ridge today and we'll try and track it."

"What will you do if you find it?" Issie asked.

"We've got long-range rifles. Our men are trained sharp-shooters," he said coolly.

"Would you like more coffee, Cameron?" Aunt Hester offered the ranger. "Issie, why don't you join us?"

Issie sat down reluctantly next to the ranger as Aunt Hester poured more coffee from the pot for herself and their guest.

"Anyway, I didn't come here just to look for your... what did you call it? A 'Grimalkin'?" the ranger told Hester as she sat down again. "You know the Conservation

Trust has been concerned for some time now about the damage the Blackthorn Ponies are causing to the native wildlife."

Hester nodded.

"We've been discussing the problem for months now. The Blackthorn Hills district is rich with rare native flora. There are species of lichen and moss here that simply don't exist anywhere else in the world. It's our job as the Conservation Trust to protect the land," the ranger continued.

"But the ponies have been here for years, Cameron. Why is the problem suddenly so urgent now?" Hester asked.

"Numbers, mostly. The cold winters have usually kept the herd numbers down but the Blackthorn Ponies have been thriving for the past couple of years. There's twice as many as there used to be. It looks like we have no alternative but to undertake the cull immediately."

Aunt Hester looked shocked. "You realise that as the chairwoman of the Save The Blackthorn Ponies Group I'll be fighting any action you plan to take at the highest level—"

Cameron cut her off. "Hester, we've been through all this a million times already and you know it. I'm not here to ask your permission. This cull has been debated and now it's been officially rubber-stamped. There's nothing you can do any more. Telling you today was only a formality. I thought you'd want to know since the herd often run on your land. We'll have our men up here next week to get the job done."

"What are you talking about?" Issie squeaked. "What do you mean by a cull?"

The ranger looked up at Issie. His face was grave. "You have to understand that these Blackthorn Ponies are hard to catch and almost impossible to manage even if we could get our hands on them, Isadora. We need to get them off the land, and as far as the Conservation Trust is concerned, that leaves us with just one solution. We'll have to shoot them."

There was silence in the kitchen for a moment. Issie looked at the ranger to see whether he was joking, but his eyes met her with a deadly serious gaze.

"Aunty Hess!" Issie gasped. "You can't let them! This is your land! They can't shoot all those beautiful horses! You can't let him kill them! You just can't!"

Hester looked distressed. "Do you think I haven't fought this tooth and nail, Issie? I know how upset you must be; I'm upset too. This debate has been raging a long time now and our action group have fought this all the way, but now it seems like this may be the only solution. Cameron is right. These ponies are destroying rare wildlife – species that may not survive for much longer. If we can't stop them – if we can't catch them – then this may be the only solution."

"But what about the ponies? What about *their* survival?" Issie said.

"I know. I know. I wish there were a way to save them," Hester said. "Cameron has tried in the past, you know. They are fiendishly difficult to catch and it takes an expert horseman to manage them. They're wild, Isadora, not at all like your typical riding ponies. And even if we could save the herd, what on earth would we do with them all?"

"Still, there must be something we can do, Aunty Hess!" Issie insisted. "What about the black stallion? What if he really *is* Avignon's son?"

Aunt Hester went quiet at this. When she finally spoke she seemed enormously sad, "He's a wild stallion, Isadora. The last time you went out there he tried to kill you. I simply don't see what we can do to save him. It's too risky. Someone might get hurt."

"Honestly, Isadora, we wouldn't be doing this if we hadn't exhausted our options," Cameron said. "It's a very humane—"

"Humane? It's murder! These are ponies we're talking about! Beautiful ponies! Some of them are just foals! I can't believe you're doing this!" Issie turned to her aunt. "And I can't believe you won't stop him!"

And with that she stormed out of the kitchen, charged up the wide wooden stairs and ran into her room, slamming the door shut behind her.

Issie lay on her bed for a long time staring at the portrait of Avignon that hung above the fireplace, wondering what she should do. She couldn't believe her Aunt was actually agreeing with the ranger. I mean, maybe they couldn't save all the ponies, but they had to try, didn't they?

Issie stood up from her bed and walked over to the sash window that looked out over the back veranda down to the stables. Aunt Hester was right. The stallion was dangerous. The last time Issie and Blaze had faced the black horse he had tried to attack them. But really, that had been Issie's fault. She hadn't been ready for him. This time, though, she would be. She could take a spare halter, some carrots to tempt the ponies...

Issie paused for a moment. Then she walked across the room to her wardrobe and got out her jodhpurs and boots. She pulled on a light jersey over her T-shirt in case the weather turned and grabbed her backpack. She climbed out of the sash window on to the veranda of her room and was about to shimmy her way down the fire escape to the lawn when she heard voices below her.

Aunt Hester and the ranger were out on the driveway. Issie lay down on the veranda out of sight and watched as the ranger got into his Jeep and said goodbye to Aunt Hester.

Issie watched the Jeep drive away and then she waited until she was sure that Aunt Hester had gone back into the house. She couldn't risk being caught and she knew she had to hurry. If Aunt Hester knew what she was about to do she would try and stop her. It was better if Issie just left now without saying anything. By the time Hester noticed that she was gone, Issie and Blaze would be on their way. With a little luck they'd capture a pony or two and be back home again in time for dinner, and Aunt Hester would be so amazed she wouldn't have the chance to be mad at her.

Issie climbed silently down the fire escape ladder, then hid against the wall of the manor until she was sure that no one was around before making the dash across the manor lawn down to the stables.

The big wooden stable doors made such a loud screech when she opened them that Issie was sure Aunt Hester could hear them all the way back up the driveway at the house. In the gloom of the stables she checked to see if Aidan was there. Luckily he wasn't. She raced straight to the tack room, grabbing her helmet, Blaze's saddle and bridle and a spare halter off the racks that lined the wall.

"Hey, girl, it's me," she said as she unbolted the door to Blaze's stall. The chestnut mare nickered when she saw her. Issie opened the stall door and slipped inside. She gave Blaze a carrot and ran her eyes over her pony's legs. She seemed none the worse for her galloping efforts yesterday.

Issie was about to start tacking up and then she stopped. What was she doing? This was crazy. She was all alone and there were at least thirty ponies out there. She didn't even have a plan. But then, what other chance did the Blackthorn Ponies have without her? She couldn't just stand by and do nothing.

"Come on, Blaze," she said to the mare as she threw the saddle blanket across her back. "We're going for a ride."

CHAPTER 7

A shiver ran down Issie's spine as she led Blaze up through the five-bar gate on to the forest ridge track. The last time they rode the ridge track they had been forced to run for their lives. Now Issie listened keenly, alert for even the slightest sound from the trees. Apart from a few bird calls, the woods were totally silent. "There's nothing in there," Issie told herself out loud. She stepped up on to the rungs of the gate and leapt lightly into the saddle, gripping the reins to steady Blaze, who was pacing nervously underneath her.

"What is it, girl?" Issie asked. She held her breath for a moment, trying to listen again, but still she heard nothing. Her eyes scanned the woods in front of her. "It's nothing," she told herself firmly. "You're just imagining things."

Issie pushed Blaze into a trot, deciding that the mare would settle down once she began to move. "Easy girl, there's nothing there to worry about," Issie reassured her. All the same, she found herself keeping one eye on the woods beside them as they rode on.

Eventually they reached the point where the track finally veered away from the forest and travelled down into the farmland and Issie breathed a sigh of relief. "See, Blaze? No big, bad kitty chasing us this time," she said, giving her pony a pat on the neck.

As the track into the farmland flattened out, Issie pushed the mare into a canter and stood up in her stirrups as Blaze fell into a steady, swift stride. They cantered on like this for a long time and by the time they slowed back down to walk again Issie could see the peak of the green hills that surrounded Lake Deepwater in the distance.

On the lake ridge Issie pulled Blaze to a halt. The Blackthorn Ponies were there, just where she had seen them last time, grazing peacefully. Issie held Blaze back for a moment, uncertain what to do next. She didn't want to startle the herd and risk a stampede. Perhaps if she rode around to the far side of the lake where the blackthorn thicket grew she could sneak up on them under the cover of the trees.

She turned Blaze around now and rode back out of sight of the herd, down the slopes away from the lake, circling around the ridge. As they reached the point where Issie figured the blackthorn trees must be she rode Blaze back up over the crest of the hill so that they were looking down on the lake once more. The herd were still grazing happily. They had no idea that Issie was stalking them. Issie held Blaze still as she counted the horses – the buckskins and bays, pintos and greys – "…twenty-five, twenty-six, twenty-seven…" She smiled at the two foals frisking along beside their mothers. "…and the foals make twenty-nine, thirty!"

Suddenly the peaceful scene was disturbed by the shrill whinny of a horse. Issie looked up along the ridge. The stallion! Issie had been wondering where he was. She held her breath and tried to keep a grip on the reins as Blaze danced and pulled beneath her. The mare wanted to run. Issie knew how she felt. She was scared too. And there was time to run now, before the stallion came too close. This time, though, something told Issie that she should hold her ground.

The stallion's stride ate up the ground as he cantered swiftly towards them. He was just a few metres away – closer than the last time they had met – when he stopped dead in front of them. He was so close that Issie could see his flanks quivering with nerves. The stallion let out a deep snort and shook his head, but instead of charging at them as he had done last time he stepped backwards, as if uncertain what to do next.

Issie realised now that it was fear, not hatred, that had driven him to attack them when they met last time. As far as the black horse was concerned, they were strangers – they were a threat. Even now, the stallion was deciding if it was safe to be this close or if he should gather his herd and run.

Issie ran a hand down Blaze's neck. The mare was shaking with tension. Issie murmured softly to her horse now, trying to soothe her. "Easy, girl, be nice, let's see if we can make friends, eh?"

The stallion took another step forward then stretched out his strong, elegant neck and greeted Blaze nose-to-nose. But Blaze wasn't so sure she wanted to make friends. She gave a tempestuous squeal and lashed out viciously at the black horse with her front leg.

"Hey, hey, girl, it's OK," Issie kept speaking gently to her horse.

Blaze seemed to listen to Issie's soothing tone because she let the stallion touch noses with her again and this time she didn't strike out.

And then the penny dropped. Issie had ridden out here on a whim to save these ponies, and here she was, so close to the stallion. *Wouldn't Aunty Hess be thrilled?* she thought to herself, *if Blaze and I could bring him home to her?* After all, hadn't Aunty Hess been convinced that the black horse was the son of Avignon, her own beloved Swedish Warmblood? If Issie was going to save just one horse from this herd, if that was all she could do, then it had to be this horse. She knew that now.

As the big black drew in close again, trying to touch noses with Blaze once more, Issie saw her chance. She unhooked the rope attached to the halter on her saddle and leant over to slip it gently, carefully over his neck. Nearly there, nearly... Issie held her breath as she leant in closer to the black horse. The stallion kept a wary eye on Issie but he didn't flinch.

"Steady, boy, it's OK," Issie said. Suddenly the stallion felt the rope against his neck and realised what was happening. He startled backwards and Issie, who had been intent on her mission, found herself losing her balance. As she made a grab for Blaze's mane to keep herself from falling she felt herself lose her hold on the halter and it slipped out of her hands and fell to the ground.

"Damn," she cursed under her breath. She had

no choice but to dismount and get it back.

Carefully, slowly, Issie climbed off Blaze's back, trying not to spook the black horse with any sudden movements as she dismounted and edged over to pick up the halter lying in the grass. All the while as she moved, she kept talking to the stallion, her voice steady and low. For a moment, the horse stood there calmly, his ears swivelling as he listened to her. Then, suddenly, he decided that he had had enough. He backed away from Issie and Blaze, wheeled about and set off at a gallop towards the herd.

At the same moment Issie, who had been preoccupied with trying to reach the halter, realised she was no longer holding on to Blaze's reins.

"Blaze!" Issie leapt forward and made a grasp at the reins, but Blaze was spooked now. She backed away from her, confused and panic-stricken. Issie lunged once more in a last desperate attempt to catch her horse as Blaze snorted in surprise and then turned and broke into a canter, following the stallion across the tussock grass, heading towards the herd.

"Blaze! No!" Issie's voice was a rasp in her throat as she shouted desperately after the mare.

Issie began to run after her, but the sudden movement of the two horses had frightened the rest of the wild herd and now they too began to scatter. As Issie sprinted across the tussock grass she found herself surrounded by Blackthorn Ponies, all of them in a blind panic. The herd were on the move and none of them wanted to be left behind.

Issie had been worried about Blaze but now she found herself fighting for her own life as she was forced to duck and weave her way through the panicky herd. The ponies seemed to be all around her now and they were in a frenzy, not knowing or caring that they might run over the girl who was in their path. Issie let out a shriek as a little bay pony narrowly missed colliding with her and she had to make a leap to get out of the way in time. As she did so she lost her footing and stumbled on a rock. She crouched down, instinctively curling into a tight ball, and managed somehow to wedge herself into the small hollow beside a large rock. The next thing she knew there was a rush of air and noise overhead and the sky above her became a thrashing, boiling mess of hooves as the herd came right over the top of her. Issie squealed and put her hands over her head. The noise around her was deafening.

By the time Issie was sure it was safe to stand up again the ponies were miles away and running up the ridge that led away from the lake. She had lost sight of Blaze completely. Where was she?

Issie held her breath and scanned the horizon, her heart beating like a drum in her chest. Where was her horse?

There! Blaze was running right near the front of the herd. Issie could see her flaxen mane and tail streaming out in the wind, her head held high as she galloped. Suddenly Blaze stopped, wheeled about and looked back towards the lake. She seemed to be searching anxiously, as if she knew she was lost and she was trying to find Issie again.

"Blaze!" Issie called out. "I'm over here! Blaze!" She cupped her hands to her mouth and whistled, but she was drowned out by the shrill call of the black stallion as he galloped up the ridge behind the mares, driving his herd on, forcing them over the crest of the hill.

"Blaze!" Issie called out desperately again. It was no good. Blaze had turned away already. Issie watched helplessly as the horses disappeared over the rise of the hill.

"Blaze!" she cried out again, but she knew it was futile. The sound of hoofbeats was so distant now she could barely hear them. The wild ponies were gone – and Blaze had gone with them.

Issie stared at the ridge for a long time after that, unable to believe what had just happened. Then she walked back across the grass, shaking and sniffling, until she found the spot where she had dropped the halter. She reached down to pick it up and then found herself collapsing in tears on the ground next to it instead. She was in big trouble this time and she knew it. She had no way of getting her horse back. Not only that, she was stranded hours from home and no one even knew where she was.

Issie lay there in the long grass thinking about what she should do next. *Should I wait here?* she wondered. Maybe Blaze would come back again. She couldn't just leave Blaze out here with the herd. Blaze wasn't a wild horse – she had no idea how to survive in the wild. And she was still wearing her saddle and bridle. What if she got tangled in a tree or something? Besides, the black stallion was so protective of his herd he might turn on Blaze and hurt her. After all, she was an outsider. There was no way Blaze would be strong enough to fight a stallion like that. She had to follow the herd and try to get her horse back.

Issie looked at the halter lying next to her. She picked it up and stood up, surveying the ridge in front of her. Then she threw it down on the grass and flopped down next to it once more. What was she thinking? Blaze was probably miles away by now. Issie had no chance on foot. The only logical thing to do was to try to get home and get help. If she set off now, Issie figured she might reach Blackthorn Manor before nightfall.

There were two ways to get home from Lake Deepwater. She could go home the same way that she had come, along the northern ridge past the forest, but somehow taking the same route home again didn't seem like such a good idea. She might be able to outrun the Grimalkin on Blaze, but on foot it would be a different story. Besides, the woods would creep her out too much. Better to go around the loop of the Coast Road. It would be slower by an hour or so, but at least it was open countryside.

Issie consulted her map. The Coast Road ran right through the length of Aunt Hester's property, starting at the sea and travelling past Lake Deepwater and through acres of rolling farmland all the way back to Blackthorn Manor. To the left she could see a peek of blue ocean on the horizon. She turned to the right – it was going to be a long walk back to Aunt Hester's.

The word "road" was actually a bit grand, Issie decided as she walked along. In fact, the Coast Road was not much more than a broad dirt and gravel track. It was wide enough for a car or a truck, but it wasn't a real road. This was private land and the only people who ever drove down here would be Aidan or Hester. There was no chance of Issie hitching a lift.

After she had been walking for a couple of hours the road swerved back inland and cut a broad ribbon through lush green pasture. The sun was shining overhead, but a cool breeze stopped the day from getting too hot. Issie stopped for a moment and took off her jersey and put it in the backpack along with her helmet and the halter.

She was just hauling the pack back on to her back when she heard a noise. She looked around but she couldn't see anything. For a moment she held her breath, not moving. There it was again! It sounded like a low, rumbling growl. She scanned the horizon. The land to her right was open green pasture, but to her left there was a dense, tangled thicket of blackthorn trees, not far from the road. Issie looked at the blackthorn trees. She couldn't see anything, but she was sure she heard something. She started walking again but she had only gone a little way further down the road when she heard it once more. This time she was certain. It was a low, rumbling feline growl. The Grimalkin was in the blackthorn bushes and it was stalking her.

Looking back later, Issie realised that what she did next was dumb. But panic had gripped her. She kept walking for a moment as she tightened the straps on her backpack and then, without even daring to look back, she broke into a run and began to sprint as fast as she could.

As soon as she started running the noise behind her became louder. She could hear the Grimalkin thrashing through the undergrowth beneath the blackthorn trees, the deep, feline growl growing nearer and nearer. It was chasing her. She should never have run, she realised. She couldn't outrun it. Maybe she should try to climb a tree? But then the Grimalkin would probably just climb after her. Besides, there weren't any trees to climb! Issie could feel the pounding of her heart in her chest. She couldn't keep running like this for much longer.

Behind her now she heard the Grimalkin, getting even closer. And then she heard another noise, a noise that made her heart soar. It was the sound of hoofbeats. Too scared to slow down, Issie tried to keep running and look behind her at the same time. The sun was glaring overhead and as she squinted into the brightness it was hard to see. Was that a horse approaching her down the dirt road? Yes! It was a horse. She could see the dapple-grey coat shining like armour in the light of the afternoon sun. It was Mystic!

As the little grey gelding got nearer Issie thought fast. She stopped running and jumped on to a nearby tree stump. "Mystic!" she called out.

The grey pony swerved to follow her and as he drew close she made a flying leap for his back and scrambled quickly onboard. Mystic slowed down just for a moment while Issie regained her balance, and then he surged on again at a gallop, with Issie clinging on desperately, her hands wrapped tightly into his long, flowing mane.

"Go, Mystic!" Issie urged the horse on. She needn't have bothered though; Mystic was already stretched out running, his legs flying over the ground beneath him, his hooves striking out a frantic rhythm on the rock-hard dirt of the road.

When the dapple-grey finally slowed his stride they had left the blackthorn bushes way behind them and Issie knew that they had outrun the Grimalkin. It wasn't until Mystic began to walk and she could untangle her hands from his mane that Issie realised how much she was shaking.

"Mystic! Ohmygod! What was that thing?" Issie murmured to the little grey. She realised now, she had been so terrified of the Grimalkin that she had barely had a chance to think about the fact that her Mystic, her own special, special Mystic was back. He hadn't forgotten about her. He was still here watching over her.

Issie ran her hands down the silvery dappled neck of the little grey. The pony shook his mane and snorted. Mystic was back. Whatever the creature was in those blackthorn trees, he had saved her from it. Issie looked back up the road behind them. There was nothing there. But she knew now that the Grimalkin was still out there somewhere. And so was Blaze.

CHAPTER 8

Issie arrived back home to find the entire manor in a state of high drama. The dogs were all racing around madly on the cherry-tree lawn and Aunt Hester was standing on the veranda with Aidan and a group of men dressed in ranger's uniforms. Hester, who was doing most of the talking while the men listened and nodded, seemed to be very upset.

Issie walked across the lawn towards them. She had let Mystic go as soon as she had reached the Blackthorn Farm driveway, since she didn't want to risk him being seen by anyone. Now, as she came into view of the manor, the dogs began barking furiously and bounded up to meet her. Aidan saw her too and came running after them.

"Where have you been?" Aidan panted as he reached Issie's side. "Hester has been mad with worry. She called in the rangers. We were just about to set out with a search party."

"I know, I'm so sorry," Issie said. "I didn't mean to worry anyone. I thought I would be back home way before now."

"Back from where?" Aidan asked.

"The lake," Issie said. "I went down to the lake to look for the horses..."

"You did what?" Aidan was stunned.

"Aidan, I found the stallion and I nearly caught him! If the rest of the herd hadn't spooked him and I hadn't dropped the halter it would have all been OK, but then Blaze got scared too and she bolted and I was stuck out there in the middle of nowhere and Blaze is gone and..."

Aidan shook his head in disbelief. He looked up to see Aunt Hester approaching them, hopping along briskly on her walking cane across the lawn.

"Listen," he hissed at Issie, "don't tell her any of this! You'll never be allowed out of the manor again if she thinks you've been off hunting wild stallions. Just keep quiet and leave it to me."

"Isadora! Thank heavens you're all right!" Hester

dropped her walking stick and grabbed Issie, smothering her in a Chanel-scented bear hug. "Where on earth have you been? We've all been so worried!"

"I... umm... I ..."

"Issie went for a hack on Blaze and got thrown," Aidan said quickly.

"Really?" Aunt Hester raised an eyebrow in surprise. "You seemed pretty upset this morning. I thought perhaps you had dashed off to do something rash?"

Issie looked sideways at Aidan. "Ummm...well, I guess I was upset. So I thought I'd go for a ride to calm down. I know I should have told you that I was going out but I thought you might not let me because of the Grimalkin, so I decided to sneak out. I'm really sorry I caused so much trouble. I thought I'd be back before anyone noticed I was gone—"

"So you're back safe and sound I see!" Cameron's voice booming across the lawn interrupted her. The ranger didn't look pleased to see Issie at all. "Well that was a complete waste of our time then, wasn't it, Hester? We'll be packing up and leaving you now." The ranger glared at Issie. "You gave your aunt quite the scare young lady and wasted valuable time. I hope it won't happen again." Cameron nodded to the other rangers, who set about packing away their backpacks and walkie talkies before piling into their Jeeps and setting off down the driveway.

"Don't worry about Cameron," Hester said as she waved them goodbye. "A good search and rescue mission is what those men thrive on. They're just cross that we found you so quickly and ruined their fun!" She turned to her niece now with a serious expression. "Now, are you going to tell me what's really going on? Where is Blaze?"

"I… I went to find the wild horses and I… Blaze got spooked by the stallion and she took off. I lost her and I had to walk home again…" Issie sighed.

"Are you OK?" Hester asked, her face grave with concern.

"I'm fine, Aunty Hess. But Blaze is still out there. She's probably terrified by now. Aunty Hess, we have to go and get her!"

"She's a horse, Isadora," Hester said firmly. "She can cope with one night of freedom out there in the wild. Besides, it's too late in the day; you don't want to be out there in the dark horse-hunting. You and Aidan can take Diablo and Paris out together tomorrow morning at first light and look for her." Hester looked sternly at

Issie. "And don't you go disobeying me on this matter. No more racing off again half-cocked to rescue wild horses, OK? I know that Cameron's news about the cull must have come as a shock to you and I love that you want to save the ponies, but we must be sensible and think this through – together." She smiled at Issie. "Now let's get you inside. You need a long hot soak with some Epsom salts in the bath. You must be aching from walking all the way home."

"I guess so," Issie replied.

Issie took one last longing look up the driveway.

"Don't worry," Aidan's voice was reassuring. "We'll find her tomorrow. We'll saddle up and set off as soon as it's light. I'll meet you down at the stables at around six a.m. OK?"

"Oh, Aidan…" Issie began, "it's all my fault. Blaze is out there all by herself and the Grimalkin is out there too…" She shivered at the thought. The Grimalkin had killed meadow. What if it hurt Blaze?

"We'll get her back. I promise," Aidan said softly. "I'll see you at six."

"Aren't you going to come into the manor now and have dinner with us?" Issie asked.

"No thanks," Aidan said. "I've still got to feed the

horses. Besides, Hester is doing a roast." He pulled a face. "I've had one of her roasts before and once was enough." He smiled at Issie. "I'm really glad you're OK, Issie. I was… I mean, your aunt was worried about you." And with that, Aidan waved a hasty goodbye as he turned and set off down the driveway.

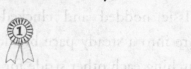

When Issie arrived at the stables the next morning Aidan already had both horses tacked up and ready to go. "I'm taking Diablo, you're on Paris," he said, handing Issie the mare's reins. Aidan looked at his watch. "Ten to six," he said. "We should be at the lake in a couple of hours if we make good time along the ridge track. Come on, let's mount up."

"Stand still, Paris," Issie said as she popped one foot in the stirrup and bounced up neatly into the saddle. It felt strange to be on a horse that wasn't Mystic or Blaze. Paris felt new and totally different. She was stockier than Blaze – a Quarter Horse like Diablo, with a short neck and broad shoulders. Issie's legs wrapped around the barrel of the mare's wide belly. She looked down at the golden palomino and hesitated for a moment.

"She's a lovely ride; you'll have no trouble with her. She's Hester's favourite." Aidan smiled.

The dawn light was turning the sky pink on the horizon as Aidan led the way through the gate on to the ridge track. "Are you ready?" Aidan asked. He was having trouble holding Diablo back; the piebald wanted to go.

Issie nodded and clucked Paris on, settling the mare into a steady pace beside Diablo, the two horses matching each other stride for stride.

They cantered on in silence all the way along the ridge. Occasionally Issie cast a wary eye at the forest next to them, but it was quiet. There was no sign of the Grimalkin. Issie stood up in her stirrups and leant low over the Paris's neck as she cantered. The sun had risen now and the palomino looked even more beautiful bathed in golden morning light.

It wasn't until they were past the forest and heading down into the farmland that Aidan finally slowed Diablo to a trot and they were able to talk.

"Thanks for coming with me to find Blaze," Issie said to him.

Aidan shrugged. "That's OK. I don't think Hester would have let you ride back out again on your own and anyway, it's kind of fun. I don't get to do much hacking out these days; I have too much farm work to do."

"Oh," Issie said, "I see. I'm really sorry. I know you have loads of work and better things to do than go looking for my horse—"

"That wasn't what I meant," Aidan stopped her. "I just meant… I'm having a really good time."

"Me too." Issie smiled. "But you have a big movie coming up, don't you? Aunty Hess says you're really busy with trick-training the horses."

Aidan smiled. "Hester worries too much. Most of her horses are totally ready – they don't need any more training. Take Diablo here," Aidan said, "he knows every trick in the book. He can climb stairs, count to ten, dance a waltz and take a bow at the end. Hester taught him all of that and I guess she's trained me too," he laughed. "She knows a few things about convincing animals and people to do whatever she wants."

Aidan gave Diablo a pat on his neck. "Hey, do you want to see one of his tricks?" Issie nodded.

"Here we go then!" Aidan suddenly pushed Diablo on into a canter. Issie pulled Paris up to a halt to watch as the piebald cantered a circle in front of her. Aidan waved over his shoulder to Issie.

"Watch this!" He grinned. While Diablo was still

cantering, Aidan quickly swung one leg over the back of the saddle so that he was standing up in the stirrup, balancing on one side of the horse and clinging to the saddle with both hands. Diablo kept cantering smoothly as if there was nothing at all unusual about having his rider hanging off the saddle like a performing monkey. As they circled once more, Aidan crouched down. Now Issie couldn't even see him as he rode past her on the circle. He was hanging on so low he was hidden behind Diablo, and the horse looked totally riderless as he cantered by. Then she saw Aidan appear, hanging upside down now, dangling underneath the horse's belly. He cantered around once more, clinging on with just one hand. With the other hand he reached all the way down to the ground and as he raced past he snatched up a wild daisy. He swung himself gracefully back up into the saddle and pulled hard on Diablo's reins. The gelding reared up dramatically, thrashing the air with his front legs. Then he came down to the ground again, snorting and prancing, clearly pleased with his performance. Aidan rode up to Issie and handed her the daisy.

"Wow!" Issie grinned, taking the flower from Aidan and reaching forward to tuck it into Paris' bridle behind the horse's ears. "That was incredible!"

"Cowboy tricks!" Aidan smiled. "It's just like in those Western movies. You know, when the cowboy hides by riding low on the side of the horse so the other cowboys don't even know he's there to shoot? Diablo is great at all the cowboy tricks. Hester even taught him to play dead when a gun is fired; that's how she broke her leg. He dropped to the ground and she got pinned underneath him by mistake."

"I know, she told me," Issie said.

"So, Hester says that Blaze knows a few tricks too?" Aidan asked.

"She can't do anything as fancy as Diablo, but she can bow. She learnt that when she was in the El Caballo Danza Magnifico," Issie said. "And she always comes when I whistle."

"Well, that trick may come in handy," Aidan said. "There's a whole lot of land out here. You may have to do a fair bit of whistling before we find your horse."

Issie looked up ahead of her. Aidan was right. Blackthorn Farm went for hundreds of miles in every direction. How on earth were they ever going to find her horse? It was like looking for a needle in a haystack. Issie was about to say as much when she heard a shrill whinny carrying clear and sharp in the morning air. Could it be Blaze? She looked up to where the sound was coming from. Ahead of her, on the horizon to the far left of the valley, she saw the grey shape of a pony, his dapples flashing in the brilliant sunshine. She squinted hard and tried to look again. The horse had disappeared, but she knew she wasn't seeing things. It was Mystic. He was trying to tell her to follow him. He was leading her to Blaze.

"This way!" she said confidently to Aidan. "I heard a horse; we need to go this way."

As they cantered on through green pasture, Issie kept checking the horizon for the little grey gelding. Sometimes she would see Mystic just up ahead of her, as if he were waiting for her to join him. But as soon as she got close enough the little dapple-grey would run again, always staying ahead of her, guiding her on.

They had ridden for several miles like this when Issie finally rode up to the brow of the hill and looked down the other side. When she saw a horse in the valley below at first she assumed it was Mystic. Then she realised it was one of the grey mares, the one with the little black foal at her feet. Next to the grey mare grazed the chestnut skewbald, the buckskin and a couple of bays.

"Aidan!" Issie called back excitedly over her shoulder. "Aidan, we've found the herd!"

As Aidan drew Diablo up next to her, Issie scanned the horses, looking frantically for Blaze. The chestnut mare and the black stallion were nowhere to be seen.

"Aidan. She's not here!" Panic rose in Issie's voice. Where was Blaze? Had something happened to her beloved pony?

"She'll be here. Stay calm," Aidan said.

Just as he said this, over the brow of the hill came Blaze.

Issie was relieved to see that Tom Avery's much-loved cross-country saddle was still on her back. The saddle had slipped a bit to the left and Blaze's reins were broken and dangling loose around her legs, but otherwise everything looked OK. As for Blaze, she looked just fine. She cantered along with her head held high and called out once more, a high shrill whinny. This time another horse answered her call.

Now the black stallion came into view. His enormous strides swallowed up the ground as he caught up to Blaze. Issie was struck once more by the beauty of the black horse.

"Isn't he beautiful?" Issie said to Aidan.

"I can't believe it. He's just like Avignon – except he's jet black!" Aidan said.

"Do you think so?" Issie said.

"Absolutely. Hester will go wild when she sees him," Aidan said. He was transfixed by the big black horse and couldn't take his eyes off him.

"What do you mean?" Issie said.

"Come on, Issie. You said yourself that you nearly caught him the other day. And now he's made friends with Blaze it should be easy. You said you wanted to save him, Issie. Well this is your chance. We can do this together. We can bring the black back home. What do you say?"

Issie looked at Aidan. "Do you really mean it?" She said.

Aidan grinned. "Uh-huh!"

Issie grinned back. "Then let's do it!" She felt a tingle of excitement run down her spine. This time they were going to catch the black horse, and she knew it. She had a plan.

CHAPTER 9

There was no time to lose. The horses still hadn't seen them, but to keep the element of surprise on their side they would have to move fast.

"Over there, behind those trees!" Issie instructed Aidan. To their right was a small copse of blackthorn bushes, perfect for hiding out of the stallion's line of sight. Issie and Aidan clucked Diablo and Paris into a canter and within a few strides the horses were behind the trees.

"What now?" Aidan asked.

"Now it's time to get my horse back," Issie said. She jumped down off Paris and peered through the trees, handing Aidan the reins. Then she cupped her hands around her mouth and blew – a shrill, high-pitched whistle.

Issie and Aidan waited in silence. Nothing.

"Try again," Aidan said. But before Issie could raise her hands to her mouth, they heard the sound of hoofbeats.

"Blaze," Issie whispered hoarsely. Her heart was thumping in her chest. She couldn't see a thing from behind these trees. Was Blaze coming to her? She didn't dare stick her head out to look now in case the stallion saw her and spooked again. She cupped her hands once more and gave another low whistle. There was a nicker in reply this time, and then there was Blaze! The mare popped her head tentatively around the corner of the trees and Issie couldn't help but giggle.

"Well, hi there!" She grinned. She dug around in her backpack for a carrot as Blaze came all the way behind the trees to join them, nickering happily as she was reunited with her girl.

"Hey, Blaze, are you OK? I missed you!" Issie hugged her pony tight around the neck, feeding her the carrot and grasping on to the broken reins. She wasn't letting go of those again in a hurry.

Issie stood back for a moment and ran her eyes over the mare. Blaze seemed fine. She ran her hands over her body. There was hardly a mark on her.

"Good girl, I'm so glad you're OK," Issie cooed. She

led her horse back over to where Aidan was holding on to Paris and waiting for them.

Issie quickly undid Blaze's girth and slipped off her cross-country saddle. Then, still holding Blaze's reins with one hand, she reached over and undid Paris' girth and slipped the saddle off the palomino. Compared to Blaze's lightweight saddle, Paris' saddle seemed enormous. It was a stock saddle, big and bulky enough to hold the weight of a rider hanging off the side, perfect for stunt riding. She swung the saddle up into the air, throwing it on to Blaze's back.

"Steady, girl," Issie said to Blaze as she did up the girth.

"Why are you swapping the saddles over?" Aidan asked as Issie yanked the girth up and checked it one last time.

"Because I need the stock saddle to do the trick of course!" Issie said matter-of-factly to Aidan. "Now I need you to stay here and hold on to Paris. You can put Blaze's saddle on her while I'm gone. Stay hidden unless I call out for you. OK?"

"No. It's not OK!" Aidan said. "First you'd better tell me what's going on. What exactly is this plan of yours?"

"Actually, it's kind of your plan," Issie said. "I got the idea from watching you do that trick on Diablo on the way here." She turned to face Aidan. "The black stallion really likes Blaze, right? She's a part of his herd now so she can get right up close to him. But he doesn't trust me just yet. If he sees me on top of her he just might freak out and bolt." Issie paused. "But what if he didn't see me?"

"I don't understand," Aidan said. "How can you get near him without him seeing you?"

Issie put her foot in the stirrup now and mounted Blaze. She swung one leg back over the saddle, balancing like a gymnast on one side of the horse, with all her weight in one stirrup. From here, she practised crouching down and hanging off one side of the saddle, just as Aidan had done on Diablo.

"Like this," she said to Aidan. "I'm going to ride the same trick that you did on Diablo. I can do it on Blaze."

Issie practised the crouch again, then she swung her leg back up and over so she was sitting in the saddle properly once more.

"Aidan, this will work! If I hang on to the side of the saddle and stay crouched down low, I can ride Blaze up towards the stallion. He won't even know I'm there until we're right up close. Then I can slip a rope around his neck and tether him to Blaze's saddle so he can't get away."

Aidan said nothing.

"Well? What do you think?"

Issie held her breath as Aidan mulled over the idea. Finally, after a long pause, he said, "I think it sounds like the best plan we've got. You and Blaze have more chance of catching him on your own. If we all charge in there he'll just bolt. Now, let me show you how to hang off the side of your saddle properly. We don't want you getting dragged under Blaze's belly."

After a quick lesson from Aidan, who also helped fashion a lasso for her to slip over the stallion's neck, Issie mounted up again and got into position.

"Steady, Blaze," Issie said as she dropped down into a crouch against the mare's left side.

"Are you ready?" Aidan asked.

Issie nodded. She had only been in position for a couple of minutes now but already her arms ached from supporting her body weight. She could feel her fingers cramping from gripping on to the front end of the saddle with one hand and the back end with the other. She needed to do this fast before her arms gave out.

"Trot on, Blaze!" Issie whispered quietly to the mare. Blaze responded instantly to her voice aids, breaking into trot as Issie tugged on the left rein, turning the mare in the direction of the stallion.

As Blaze's trot quickened the ride got bumpier.

Just hang on, not much longer now… Issie told herself. Her arms really ached. She could feel the fingers of her left hand cramping painfully as she gripped on to the pommel. Her right hand, which was wet with sweat, was beginning to slip off the cantle…

Just as Issie felt like she was losing her grip, Blaze began to slow down and pulled up to a halt. The mare gave a keen nicker and Issie heard the sound of the stallion talking back to her. He was close. Very close. Issie couldn't see where he was, and she was too nervous to lift her head up above the saddle in case he saw her and spooked. She didn't know what to do next. She held her breath, too scared to move at all. This was crazy! She couldn't catch the stallion if she couldn't see him!

Then she realised that she could pull the same trick Aidan had done when he had picked her that flower. If she hung low enough under Blaze's belly then she'd be able to look through the mare's legs and see the stallion on the other side.

As she lowered herself down head first she felt her face flush from the rush of blood. Then, there she was, swinging upside down, dangling with her face precariously close to the ground, with just her right hand gripping the stirrup leather to keep her from falling.

Now that she was down low she could look through Blaze's legs and see the stallion. She was right. He was very close. In fact he was standing right next to Blaze. If she suddenly appeared, the stallion would be spooked for sure. How could she get close enough to slip the rope around his neck without him seeing her? She had to think fast.

Steeling her nerve, Issie unhooked the rope from the saddle and slipped her foot out of the stirrup, dropping silently to the ground. She was still hidden from the stallion's view by Blaze's body. She leant her back against Blaze's belly and took a deep breath. Stay low, that was the way to do it. She dropped into a low crouch on the ground next to Blaze, then crawled under her belly and crouched between her legs. It was a risky place to be and Issie knew it. If Blaze lashed out suddenly or even moved a hoof Issie would get kicked. She had to put her faith in her pony. Blaze knew that Issie was there; she wouldn't hurt her. Blaze didn't move a muscle as Issie edged further under her belly and got into position.

The stallion was right above her now. He was so close that Issie could reach out her hand and touch him. The big black horse lowered his head over the chestnut mare and nibbled affectionately at her shoulder. There wouldn't be a better time to do this. She had to move now!

In one swift motion Issie slipped out from underneath Blaze's belly, quickly throwing the rope around the stallion's neck, grasping the end and looping it back through the lasso.

The black horse felt the rope against his neck and suddenly noticed Issie. Startled, he reared back, taking up the slack. As he did so, Issie hurriedly tied the rope to the pommel of Blaze's saddle. Then she swiftly jammed her foot into the stirrup and threw herself desperately back up on to Blaze's back.

As the stallion reared back and pulled against her, Issie reined Blaze backwards too, asking the mare to hold her ground against the big, black horse. The stallion strained against the rope, shaking his head and trying to free himself. He gave two little bucks, going straight up in the air. But he didn't panic. It was as if he knew that struggling would get him nowhere.

"Clever boy," Issie said. "You know I've got you, don't you?"

The stallion gave a defiant toss of his head and pulled back against the rope once more, testing his limits. Then he stopped struggling against Blaze's weight and stood still. His body was quivering but he seemed almost resigned to being caught.

"Aidan!" Issie shouted out. "I've got him. Bring the halter."

Aidan rode up on Diablo, the halter in his hand. He headed towards the stallion but then decided against it and handed the halter over to Issie. "He trusts you and Blaze more than me. You do it!" Aidan instructed.

Issie nodded and rode Blaze forward, pulling up the slack on the rope in her hand as she went. When she finally reached the stallion, she managed to slip the halter quickly over his head.

"Steady boy, I've got you." She spoke softly to the horse as she refastened the rope from around his neck, attaching it to the halter instead. "All done. We've got him. I don't believe it!" She grinned over at Aidan who was watching the whole thing.

"I don't believe it either!" Aidan shook his head. "Well, well. Aren't you something, Issie Brown?"

Issie looked at the black horse, now standing peacefully beside her. "Did you see that, Aidan? He's so clever. He calmed right down as soon as he knew he was caught."

Aidan nodded. "He's a smart horse." Then he smiled at Issie. "I think it helps that he seems to be in love with your mare!"

"I know." Issie nodded. "He's happy when he's with

Blaze, isn't he? I'd better lead him home. Can you ride Diablo and lead Paris?"

"Sure," Aidan nodded, "whatever you say, horse-whisperer! Let's get him home."

As they set out along the Coast Road Issie took the lead on Blaze with the stallion trotting along beside her. Issie began to think that Aidan was right. Maybe the stallion was in love with her mare. He trotted along briskly beside her, his head held high, his tail erect.

"He's got a beautiful trot, hasn't he?" Issie shouted back over her shoulder at Aidan, who was riding a few lengths behind her, keeping Diablo and Paris well out of the stallion's reach in case he lashed out.

Aidan nodded. "Floating paces. A classic warmblood – just like Avignon. I can't wait until Hester sees him. I want to see the look on her face."

The look on Hester's face when they arrived was not at all what they had anticipated. Instead of the beaming smile they had been expecting, Hester turned white with shock. Her eyes welled with tears as she reached Issie's side. She looked up at the black horse and was very quiet for a moment. When she finally spoke her voice was shaky.

"Do you know," she said, "when I saw you all coming down the driveway just now it was like seeing a ghost. He's the spitting image of my darling Avignon!"

Hester stepped forward, reached out a hand and took the lead rope from Issie, untying it from the saddle. As Issie and Aidan watched, she cooed and clucked softly to the big, black horse. The stallion took a step towards her and Issie marvelled at her aunt's natural ease with the animal. Within moments she was stroking his nose and running her hands down his neck and over his back.

"Steady there, my lovely boy," she cooed. "You're not a bit wild, are you? Where did you come from?"

Hester smiled up at Issie now. "How clever you both are, catching him like that! Your mother would kill me of course, Isadora, if she knew I was allowing you to go out on a wild horse hunt! But how fabulous! And you were right: I have no doubt in my mind as I look at him now. He is Avignon's son. You have brought him home. Coming here was his destiny."

"Destiny! That's it!" Issie said. "Aunty Hess, you're a genius! I've been trying to think of a name for him all the way home. That's the perfect name for him. Destiny it is!"

Aunt Hester turned to the black stallion. "Do you

hear that, Destiny? You've got a new home and a new name all in one day." She smiled at Issie and Aidan. "Come on then, let's get Destiny settled in. He can go in the field next to the duck pond. It's too soon to expect him to be stabled. Besides, he would go bonkers if we kept him too near the mares!" she explained.

They all stood and watched as Destiny moved around the perimeter of the paddock, which had high fencing on every side. He trotted back and forth and let out a few high-pitched calls. Then he galloped the fence-line, charging down on the rails at the end of the paddock. For a moment it looked as if he might try to jump, but at the last moment he swerved and kept galloping. After a few laps of the field, punctuated by moments when he stopped to sniff the ground, looking for the smells of horses that had been there before, Destiny eventually settled down.

By the time Issie returned from the stables after putting Blaze away for the night, the stallion was grazing peacefully as if he had lived at Blackthorn Farm all his life.

Issie helped Aidan untack Paris and Diablo, feeding them and bedding them down for the night, then they headed back up to the manor where Aunt Hester was cooking dinner.

"What's she making us?" Issie said.

"Her famous lasagne," Aidan groaned.

"That doesn't sound so bad," Issie said optimistically.

"It's called famous lasagne because it's famous for giving you a stomach ache for three days afterwards." Aidan grinned.

As they chewed their way through the lasagne on their plates Aunt Hester quizzed them both about how they had caught Destiny. When Issie told her about the stunt-riding trick Hester whooped with delight. "I'm so glad all my trick-training got put to real use for once!" She beamed.

"Aunty Hess," Issie said as she put down her cutlery and stopped trying to hack into her lasagne crust, "please, I want to talk to you about the cull."

The table went quiet.

"Isadora, I know how you feel—" her aunt began. But Issie cut her off before she could say anything more.

"Aunty Hess, you feel the same way. I know you do! We have to stop it!"

Hester shook her head. "It can't be stopped, my dear. Don't you think I've already tried? My group, Save the Blackthorn Ponies, have been fighting Cameron on this for years now. We've won several legal wrangles, but the Conservation Trust are very hot under the collar about the damage the ponies are doing. They've done their homework and their paperwork. They took it all the way to the high court and it has been decreed that the horses must go. Cameron is a good man, he's given us loads of second chances and we've exhausted all the options. I don't see what else we can do."

Issie was about to answer back when she heard Aidan's voice speaking up next to her. "We can catch them ourselves," he said.

"What?"

"The Conservation Trust doesn't care what happens to the horses, as long as we get them off the land, right?" Aidan shrugged. "So all we've got to do is catch them."

"That's all very well, Aidan, but Cameron and his men have tried that already," Hester sighed. "Those ponies are damn near impossible to muster and you know it."

"Maybe for Cameron and his boys, but we've never tried before, have we?" Aidan replied.

"Well," Hester said considering this, "what if we do catch them? What then? We can't keep thirty more horses on this farm! Besides, these are wild horses – they're unbroken."

"Ohmygod!" Issie yelped suddenly. "I've just had

144

a really great idea. Aunty Hess! We can do it. I know someone who can help us. We're going to save the horses! Not just Destiny – all of them!"

That night, around the kitchen table, Issie laid out her plan to Hester and Aidan. After much discussion, they all agreed that it just might work. Then phone calls were made, further plans were hatched and rooms were prepared with spare beds made up with fresh linen. After all, they needed to be ready. Tomorrow, the cavalry were coming.

CHAPTER 10

Issie looked anxiously at her watch. Unbelievable! It was almost midday.

"They were supposed to be here by now. Why aren't they here?" She complained to Aidan. They were sitting together on the sofa on the upstairs balcony of the manor overlooking the cherry-tree lawn.

"Issie, calm down," Aidan said gently. "They said they'd be here by lunchtime and it's not even—"

"They're here!" Issie suddenly leapt up and left Aidan in mid-sentence as she raced back into the house and ran down the stairs.

Aidan listened to Issie's frantic footsteps on the staircase. He heard the front door swinging open and slamming shut again as Issie dashed outside. Coming towards her down the long, leafy driveway was a dark green Range Rover. Issie waved, gesturing for it to circle the lawn and pull up in the parking bay right next to the front door of Blackthorn Manor. Dust flew up from beneath the tyres as it pulled to a stop. The driver's door flew open and out stepped Tom Avery.

"Well, Isadora, I wasn't expecting this. It's quite the grand country estate, isn't it?" Avery said, looking about.

"Tom!" Issie grinned. "Thanks so much for coming—"

She was interrupted by the sound of the other doors of the Range Rover opening.

"Issie!" Stella squealed, jumping down from the passenger seat and running round to give her best friend a hug.

"Ohmygod, it is amazing here!" Kate shrieked as she hopped out of the back and ran over to join her friends. Ben and Dan emerged now too, stretching dramatically and shaking out their arms and legs.

"I feel so cramped up after that long drive! We left at five in the morning to get here!" Ben groaned.

"Oh, stop complaining!" Dan snapped at him. "You slept most of the way. You were snoring and drooling on my shoulder."

"Hi, guys," Issie beamed at them. "Thanks for coming. I really, really appreciate it."

At that moment there was a sudden yelp and a chorus of barking as Strudel, Nanook and Taxi officially announced the arrival of the new guests. The three dogs bounded out the front door to greet everyone, followed by Aunt Hester and Aidan.

"Aunty Hess! Come and meet my friends. This is Stella, Kate, Dan and Ben," Issie began her introductions. "And this is my riding instructor, Tom Avery."

"Welcome to Blackthorn Manor, everyone!" Hester said brightly. "Lovely to meet you, Tom. Isadora has told me so much about you. You know, I used to watch you ride on TV. I once saw you do a clear round in the cross-country at Burghley on that enormous bay gelding of yours…"

"Lucky Jim?" Avery said. "He was a fabulous horse. Never slowed down for a fence, mind you. I rode him in a gag, but he was still impossible to stop."

"Oh!" Issie said, spotting Aidan quietly standing behind Aunt Hester. "I haven't finished my introductions. Everyone, this is Aidan. Aidan, this is Tom, Stella, Kate, Dan and Ben."

"Hello…" Aidan stepped out from behind Hester and gave them all a shy wave.

"Hi, Aidan!" they all replied.

Stella, who was boggling at Aidan, leant over and whispered rather too loudly in Issie's ear. "That's him? Issie, I told you so! I knew it. He's totally gorgeous!" Issie elbowed Stella roughly. "Ow! What did you do that for?" Stella said. Issie glared at her, willing Stella to shut up.

"Aidan helped me catch Destiny," Issie said. She kept an eye on Stella as she said this. She was terrified her friend might say something else. She would be so embarrassed if Aidan thought she had a silly crush on him or something.

"I'm dying to see him!" Kate said. "I've never even seen a stallion before. I bet he's beautiful."

"We'll show you to your rooms and then you can meet the horses." Hester smiled brightly. "Come on in – we're all ready for you."

While Aidan showed Avery and the boys to their rooms Issie took Stella and Kate on a whirlwind tour of Blackthorn Manor, showing them the vast ballrooms downstairs, the grand dining room and the wood-panelled billiards room.

"This must be what a princess' house looks like!" Stella gasped as she stroked the brilliant green feathers of one of the stuffed pheasants and stared up at the oil paintings of racehorses on the walls.

"This is most amazing room I've ever been in," Kate agreed as she cast her eyes around the ornate ceilings hung with sparkling crystal chandeliers.

"It's so good that you're here! I still can't believe it!" Issie beamed at her friends. "I'm really sorry for dragging you away like this. I know you were doing the summer dressage series and everything…"

"What? Are you nuts! We couldn't wait to leave," Stella said. "Natasha was driving us crazy. She was winning by like, a million miles on that new horse of hers. Which is fine, except after every competition she would go over the leader board in the clubroom with a highlighter pen and highlight her scores so that everyone could see how much she's winning by and—"

"Oh, just forget about it, Stella! We're here now!" Kate shut her up.

"Come on" Issie told them. "You can unpack your bags later. Let's go to the stables. I can't wait for you to meet Destiny."

Dan, Ben and Avery were already at the stables when the girls arrived. They were watching over the rails as Destiny paced and fretted along the fenceline. With an audience to watch him, Destiny broke out of his high-stepping trot into a canter, tossing his head as he circled the paddock.

"What do you think, Tom?" Issie said.

"He has terrific paces," Avery mused. "Hester might be right about Avignon. This horse certainly moves like a warmblood. Does he have a brand?"

Issie shook her head. "No, there are no markings on him. Hester thinks that Avignon might have escaped at some point and bred with a Blackthorn Pony."

"Perhaps…" Avery said. "But you say he's not as wild as the rest of them?"

"He let me put a halter on him and lead him back to the farm," Issie replied.

"It makes no sense," Avery said. "A horse like this, left to roam wild. How did he get there?"

Destiny stopped cantering now and stood at the end of the paddock nearest the stables. He let out a shrill, high whinny and a moment later another horse returned his call.

"That's Blaze!" Issie smiled. "Come on, I'd better go and check on her and then you can meet your horses."

"Today is Wednesday and the cull is due to happen on Friday. It's too late to ride out today, of course, so that only leaves tomorrow to muster the herd," Hester explained as they all walked together to the stables. "We thought if we allocated each of you a horse now then you'd be all set and ready to go first thing

151

in the morning. We're aiming for a six a.m. start."

Issie pulled a crumpled piece of paper out of her pocket. "Right!" she said. "This is the list of horses and riders for tomorrow's muster. I'm on Blaze, obviously, and Aidan has Diablo – he's the piebald in the last stall. Stella and Kate – you're on Paris and Nicole – the twin palominos. Ben is on Scott – he's the skewbald in that stall over there to your left. Dan is riding Tornado – he's the dark bay hunter in the last stall. He's the one Aunty Hess usually rides…"

Issie looked back down at her list. "And Tom, you're on Titan," Issie said mischievously. "I think you'd better come over here and meet him."

Issie pulled a face over her shoulder at Stella and the others as she walked with Avery to the first stall in the row. They all gathered round as Avery opened the Dutch door. He looked puzzled. "I don't understand. There's no horse in here," he said.

"Yes there is!" Issie laughed. She unbolted the bottom half of the door and there was little Titan, all nine hands of him, looking up at them from underneath his enormous shaggy brown forelock.

Everyone started laughing as Avery strode over to the miniature pony and stood over him. Titan was so tiny that he barely reached Avery's hip. Everyone laughed even harder.

"I think you may have to find me a slightly larger mount, Isadora," Avery said, trying to keep a straight face.

"I've got just the thing right next door," Issie said. "You can ride Dolomite."

If the riders had been laughing hard before, they hooted and wailed now at the sight of the enormous eighteen hand Dolomite next to the tiny miniature pony.

"Haven't you got something somewhere in between these two?" Avery asked.

"Actually, no. I wasn't joking. I was hoping you'd ride Dolomite," Issie said. "I know he looks huge but Aunty Hess says he's very well schooled."

"Well, I'm certainly not riding Titan, so I guess I have no choice, do I?" Avery smiled.

With the horses all fed and the tack sorted for the next day they locked up the stables for the night and headed back up to Blackthorn Manor. Over dinner the riders looked at the map of Blackthorn Farm as Aunt Hester filled them in on the details of the impending cull.

"Cameron is assembling his team now. Friday is D-day," Hester said gravely. "It doesn't leave us much time… And then, of course, once we've got the herd back here that leaves us with an even bigger problem. What on earth are we going to do with them?"

"That's where you come in, Tom," Issie said. "When Aunty Hess told me that these horses were wild with no homes to go to I suddenly realised that I had the solution all along. You work for the International League for the Protection of Horses. You can take the wild horses and find them new homes – good homes where they'll be cared for properly by owners that love them. You can do it, can't you?"

Avery looked serious. "What you're asking is no small feat, Isadora. Your Aunt is right – these are wild ponies born and bred and they won't be easy to school. They'll be a handful for even an experienced horseman." Avery saw Issie's face fall at this news.

"Hey now! I never said it couldn't be done – just that it wouldn't be easy. Of course the ILPH will take these horses. I've been in touch with them and organised everything. The Blackthorn Ponies will be trucked to the ILPH fields after they're mustered. We'll keep them there and feed them up, break them in and give them a bit of basic schooling before we find them new homes. All the prospective owners will have to pass our checks before they can re-home a Blackthorn Pony, of course. These are very special ponies – you can be sure we'll be keeping an eye on them once they have new owners."

"Thanks, Tom," Issie smiled, "they're really amazing ponies. Wait until you see them."

"We should all get an early night," Aidan advised them as he headed back out the door and home to his cottage. "We'll need to be ready to mount up by six a.m. when it's light enough to ride."

"Who made him the boss?" Dan muttered as Aidan left.

"Aidan is the farm manager. He's a really good trick rider and he knows what he's doing," said Issie.

"Yeah, well, he's not that much older than us and he doesn't get to boss us around," Dan said sulkily. "Anyway, goodnight. I was going to bed anyway."

"What's up with him?" Issie asked Ben.

Ben rolled his eyes. "Duh, Issie! Think about it. Maybe he's jealous? You've been going on and on about Aidan this and Aidan that ever since we got here!"

Issie was shocked. "I don't know what you're talking about!"

"Yeah, right," Ben said. "I'd better get to bed now too. It's a big day tomorrow."

Could Dan really be jealous of Aidan? thought Issie.

"Of course he is!" Stella laughed when Issie asked her this. The girls were sitting on Issie's four-poster bed having hot chocolates with marshmallows as a pre-bedtime treat.

"I'm jealous too!" Kate said. "I mean, Aidan is so cool. Have you noticed how his hair kind of dangles over his eyes like that? How does he even see where he's going?"

Issie smiled at this. She had noticed Aidan's hair. It was kind of cute how it hung over his face, hiding his blue eyes. "But it's not like he likes me or anything," she protested.

"Issie! Haven't you noticed that he's always hanging around?"

"That's because he works here, Stella," Issie sighed.

"Anyway, we're supposed to be having an early night…" Issie started, then hesitated. She leapt to her feet and ran to the window.

"Issie, what are you—?" Stella began, but Issie hushed her.

"Listen!" Issie said. "Do you hear that?"

The three girls froze for a moment in silence. There was nothing to hear. The night air was completely quiet. And then, just when Issie thought she must have been imagining it, she heard the noise again. There it was! Even louder now. A deep rumbling, like the growl of a big cat.

The girls held their breath. There was silence again for a moment and then the feline rumble could be heard once more. Issie felt the hairs rise on the back of her neck. The growl sounded close. The animal must be right outside.

"Ohmygod!" Stella breathed. Her face was deathly pale, her eyes were wide with fear. "What is that?"

"That," said Issie, "is the Grimalkin."

CHAPTER 11

So much for an early night! Arming themselves with a torch, the girls had raced outside in search of the Grimalkin and they were now huddled together on the back veranda of the manor.

"Hurry up, Stella!" Issie hissed.

"I'm trying to make this work… ahh, got it!" Stella switched the torch on and shone the beam out into the inky blackness. The torchlight flickered over the lawn, the magnolia trees, the fishpond and then suddenly, caught in the beam were a pair of yellow eyes. Kate let out a scream and grabbed at Stella's arm.

The yellow eyes came closer. In the shadows a huge black animal loomed, bearing down on them.

"Wait a minute…" Issie took the torch off Stella and

shone it once more on the animal. She heaved a sigh of relief. It wasn't the Grimalkin.

"You guys – it's just Nanook!" Issie said.

Nanook bounded towards them now, wagging her tail happily.

"Nanook! You scared us half to death!" Stella growled at the dog.

"It's not her fault," Issie defended her. "That growling that we heard earlier – I'm sure that was the Grimalkin. Nanook probably heard it too; that's why she's out here."

"Well, it doesn't look like there's anything here now," Kate said, shining the torch over the garden and checking once more. As she shone the beam one more time across the lawn, though, there was something moving, coming towards them. A dark shape was moving swiftly across the grass, heading straight for the manor...

"Aidan!" Issie cried out with relief.

"What's going on?" Aidan asked as he ran up the stairs to join them. "What are you all doing outside?"

"We heard a noise," Stella said. "It sounded like a cat growling."

"Me too," Aidan said. "I was in bed when the horses in the stable block suddenly started kicking up a fuss. I went outside to check them and then I heard it.

I was just coming up to the house to make sure that everything was all right up here."

"Are the horses all OK?" Issie asked.

Aidan nodded. "They're locked in and there's nothing there. Whatever it was must have been scared off."

"So it's gone?" Stella sounded disappointed. "I wish we'd seen it!"

"No. You really don't," Issie said softly, remembering what the Grimalkin had done to poor Meadow.

"Issie's right," Aidan agreed. "You don't want to come face-to-face with this thing. We're just lucky it hasn't hurt any of the animals this time."

Aidan looked at the girls. "Listen, let me take the torch and I'll take the dogs and make one last round of the manor and the stables to make sure its gone. You guys go back to bed and get some sleep."

Kate reluctantly handed Aidan the torch and the three girls went back inside.

"I wish we'd gone with Aidan to check the grounds. I really wanted to actually see the Grimalkin," Stella grizzled as they walked back up the stairs to their bedrooms.

"Me too," Kate agreed.

"You guys, this is serious!" Issie said. "You don't know what this animal can do. The night when Meadow was killed I saw it on the fence in the moonlight, walking along the top of the rails. And then when I saw what it had done to Meadow. It ripped her throat open – it was horrible."

"Do you think it was the same animal that chased you on Blaze?" Stella asked.

"Uh-huh. It's really fast. Blaze was totally galloping and it nearly caught us," Issie said.

"This whole Grimalkin thing is starting to creep me out," Kate said with a shiver.

Sleep was a good idea. But it wasn't easy. Issie lay awake for a long time. When she did finally sleep she dreamt of Mystic. In her dream she was riding the little grey gelding down by Lake Deepwater. The cull had started and the gunmen were tracking the wild herd. She was looking for Blaze and Destiny, trying desperately to find them. There was confusion, horses running everywhere and then suddenly a shot rang out. She saw a horse fall as the gun fired and she began to gallop on Mystic towards the black shape lying on the ground. In her heart she knew the animal lying there was dead. But which horse was it? It was hard to see...

"Mystic?" Issie murmured. "Mystic, what's happening?"

The noise of her alarm clock woke her and she sat up in bed, her heart racing. She felt a wave of relief as she realised it had all been a dream. The bedside clock was flashing – 5:30 A.M. Issie rolled out of bed. It was dark outside but she could already see the faint blush of the sun as it crept up the horizon. She pulled on her jodhpurs and a jersey and headed downstairs for breakfast. Dream or no dream, this was mustering day and it was time to ride.

The riders barely spoke in the darkness of the stables as they prepared their horses. Once they were all saddled up, Aidan gathered everyone together outside near the gate for a team talk.

"We'll take it slowly along the ridge. No cantering – keep the horses to a trot," Aidan instructed. "We need them fresh for the muster, so let's not tire them out."

"Is this where the Grimalkin attacked you?" Stella whispered to Issie, looking up at the forest next to the ridge track. "Are you sure it's not still in there? Maybe we should go the other way along the Coast Road instead."

Issie shook her head. "It's much faster to the lake this way. Besides, the second time I got chased I was on the Coast Road anyway..." Issie realised as soon as she said this that she should have shut up. No one knew she had been chased by the Grimalkin twice now.

"What?" Stella looked at Issie. "You got chased twice? What happened?"

Issie hesitated, "Well… I'm not sure it was the Grimalkin that time. You know, I was out there on my own because Blaze had run away. I was probably just imagining things."

Stella nodded at this. "It must have been awful. Losing Blaze, I mean. You must have been so worried. And poor Blaze – out there all alone!"

Issie nodded and turned to her horse, putting an arm around Blaze's neck and stroking the crest of her honey-coloured mane. "It's so good to have you home again, girl. I don't want anything to ever happen to you. Not ever."

Issie's mind flashed back again to the dream she had last night. She had heard a shot and seen a horse fall to the ground. Had it been Blaze that had fallen? She was about to tell Stella about the dream, but she changed her mind. *It was just a dream,* she told herself, *forget about it.*

"Which horse am I on?" Stella whispered to Issie. "Is this one Paris or Nicole? How do you tell them apart? I'm—"

"Hello? Are you all listening up the back there?" Avery

called out rather pointedly to Stella. "Because Aidan is about to explain the plan for the muster before we set off."

Aidan took some sheets of paper out of his pocket and began to pass them around to each of the riders. "It's a map of Blackthorn Farm," he explained. "The herd have been seen at Lake Deepwater twice now so it looks like that's the best place to start. We'll track them down and then drive them back along the Coast Road to Blackthorn Manor. There's only seven of us and thirty horses so we'll have to spread out behind them and keep the herd moving."

"What if we don't find them?" Kate asked.

"It's Thursday now. Tomorrow they start the cull. We don't have a choice. We've got to find them," Aidan replied.

The horses and riders set off at a steady trot along the ridge track. Stella and Kate rode side by side on the two identical palominos. Aidan rode at the front on Diablo, with Avery next to him on the enormous Clydesdale, Dolomite.

As the horses all settled into a stride, Issie heard hoofbeats behind her and turned around to see Dan riding up next to her.

"Hi," he said uncomfortably.

"Hi," she replied.

"So… it's pretty cool, isn't it? Riding out to muster some wild horses. You don't get to do this kind of thing at pony club," Dan said.

"Uh-huh," Issie said. "Thanks for coming to help."

"No problem," Dan said. He paused for a moment and then he added, "When I heard you'd gone away to your aunt's I thought I'd have to go through the whole summer holidays without seeing you."

"Yeah, I figured I'd just see you again when I got back to pony club," Issie said.

"I know, I know…" Dan trailed off. Then he spoke again. "Hey, Issie. Can I ask you something?"

"Uh-huh. What?" Issie said.

"Is Aidan your boyfriend?"

Issie felt her heart begin to race. She looked at Dan. Was it true what Ben and Stella had said? Was Dan jealous of Aidan?

"I don't think so… I mean… no. No, he's not," Issie stuttered.

Dan's face broke into a huge grin. "Good," he said. And with that, he clucked his horse into a canter and rode off to catch up with Ben.

Issie spent the rest of the ride to the lake feeling confused. She was still puzzling over what Dan had said to her as the riders came over the green ridge of the hill and looked down into the valley of Lake Deepwater below. Issie's heart sank. The horses weren't there.

"Oh well, so much for plan A," Stella said as they scanned the lake. "Where to from here?"

"We'll ride around the lake and along the Coast Road to the very end, to Preacher's Cove." Aidan instructed as he rode Diablo down towards the lake. "This way!" he called over his shoulder for the rest of them to follow him.

"It's turning into a bit of a wild-horse chase," Ben said. Then he turned to the others and grinned at his own joke. Stella, Kate and Issie all groaned.

There was no sign of the herd on the ride to Preacher's Cove either.

"Needle in a haystack if you ask me!" Dan sulked as they reached the top of the hill. Below them was Preacher's Cove, a tiny beach wedged in between steep cliffs on either side. The sand was sparkling white, the sea was brilliant blue, there was kikuyu grass for the horses to graze on and low-hanging pohutukawa trees right down near the beach to tether the ponies underneath for shade while they ate.

"We're going to break here for lunch," Aidan said as he rode Diablo down the hill.

"I thought we were supposed to be mustering horses,

not having a picnic," Dan grumbled, following him.

At the bottom of the cove the riders dismounted and loosened their girths.

"Once we've eaten, we'll ride back along the Coast Road towards Blackthorn Manor," Aidan said. "If we stick to the road we'll have a good view. We might be able to see them from there—"

"And if we don't see them?" Dan interrupted him.

Aidan shrugged. "Then we keep looking."

"It doesn't sound like much of a plan," Dan said.

"Do you have a better one?" Aidan turned on him.

"Hey, listen, you two," Issie said.

"It wasn't me…" Dan began.

"No. I mean it. Listen," Issie said. "Shut up and listen!"

The riders realised what she meant now. They stopped talking and sat there for a moment in silence.

"Do you hear that?" Issie asked.

"Yup," Stella replied.

"Hear what?" said Dan.

"Hoofbeats" the girls replied.

They could all hear it now as the sound grew louder. They were coming closer.

"It looks like we won't have to find the Blackthorn Ponies," Issie said. "They've found us."

CHAPTER 12

As the sound of hoofbeats came closer the riders sprang into action.

"They're coming down into the cove." Aidan leapt up again and began tightening Diablo's girth, "We can corral them here and then drive them home." He turned to Avery. "If you take the girls and ride up the hill, you can take cover in the trees up there and then circle around behind the herd and trap them in the cove. I'll stay here with the boys and once they're trapped we'll try and herd them back up the hill again."

"Is there any other way out of the cove?" Avery asked.

Aidan shook his head. "The Coast Road is the only way in or out. If they come down here then we should have them trapped."

Avery took the lead on Dolomite as the horses galloped up the hill. Issie marvelled at just how fast the big draught horse could move. With each giant stride the Clydesdale swallowed up the ground, leaving Issie and the others galloping furiously just to keep up. They were halfway to the top when Avery directed them towards a massive fallen tree that was blocking one side of the road. The instructor pulled the draught horse up to a halt.

"This would be the best place to position ourselves. We can use this tree as a road block to help us pen the horses in," Avery said. "Those trees there should provide enough cover. We'll duck behind them, wait for the herd to go past and then we'll come out and form a road block – we'll have them trapped."

Unfortunately the clearing behind the trees wasn't big enough to fit four horses – especially when one of those horses was an eighteen-hand Clydesdale.

"Hey! I was going to go there! Move over – I don't have any room!" Stella squawked.

"I'm trying!" Issie snapped back.

"Just get your horses out of sight as much as possible and keep quiet!" Avery muttered. He had backed Dolomite in behind the biggest tree but the horse was so huge his rump stuck out one side and his neck stuck out the other.

"This is hopeless!" Stella groaned.

"Don't worry. Just stay still and keep quiet until the herd has gone past," Avery hissed.

The riders tried to hold their horses steady as the sound of hoofbeats thundered in their ears. Issie held her breath as she saw the first horse, the buckskin mare, enter the cove over the crest of the hill. She kept a tight grip on the reins, holding Blaze perfectly still as the mare galloped past without noticing the riders hidden behind the trees. Then the rest of the herd followed behind the buckskin down into the cove. Issie watched the blur of ponies pass by. There was the pretty grey mare with the black foal at her feet, and the chestnut skewbald mare with her matching foal, both tearing past at full gallop.

"Ohmygod! Look at those foals! Aren't they just the cutest things you've ever seen?" Stella whispered.

"I like the little black one," Kate said.

"Really? I think the chestnut and white one is the prettiest. Look at his little face, with that cute white blaze and that fluffy white and chestnut mane..."

"Girls! Get your heads back in the game. We've got a job to do," Avery growled at them.

"Is that the whole herd?" he asked Issie.

"I think so." Issie nodded.

"Right then, let's spread out and cover the road. We need to block their path out of the cove," Avery instructed.

The riders began to move back out from behind the trees with Avery directing them into position next to the fallen tree.

"Issie! Can you see what's going on down there?" Stella asked. "I can't see from where I am."

Issie looked down the hill. "They've stopped," she said. "They're settling down and grazing by the trees. I think I can see Aidan on Diablo… he's getting closer to them…"

"I can't stand it!" Stella said. She pushed Paris into a canter and left her position to join Issie so that she could see what was going on.

"Ohmygod!" Stella shrieked. "They've seen Aidan. They're off! They're coming back this way!"

Clouds of dust rose up from the dirt road as the herd headed back up the hill. The ponies were in full gallop, their eyes wild with fear. They were heading straight for Issie and the others.

"Move back into position NOW, Stella!" Avery yelled at her.

"It's no good, Tom, they're moving too fast. We'll get trampled!" Kate shouted.

Avery shook his head. "No. Just hold your ground. They'll stop," he said.

Issie was trying to hold her ground but as the horses got closer Blaze became more and more crazed. She gripped the reins as tightly as she could and held the mare steady.

"Easy, girl. Stand still. They're going to stop in a minute. Any minute now… I promise," Issie breathed.

"Tom?" Stella's voice was tense. "Tom? They're not stopping…"

"Trust me, Stella. Stay where you are," Avery said. He had positioned himself on Dolomite in the very centre of the road just beside the fallen tree. Dolomite was turned sideways so that his great bulk almost spanned the right-hand side of the road, cutting it off completely. The fallen tree blocked the road off to the left – the roots of the tree were pressed up hard against the banks of the cliff. The only way for the horses to escape was to the right of Avery and Dolomite, where Stella, Kate and Issie were all trying very hard not to panic as they manoeuvred their horses into the gap to form a barricade.

The Blackthorn Ponies were still in full gallop with the buckskin mare at the head of the herd, taking the lead.

Then suddenly the buckskin slowed to a canter.

She seemed to sense that she was penned in, that her path to freedom was blocked. Snorting and indignant, she swerved to the left towards Avery and Dolomite.

"She's going to turn around," Avery shouted to the others. "She's figured out that she's trapped and she'll lead the rest of the herd back down into the cove."

For a moment, it looked as if the little buckskin pony was going to do exactly that. Then, with a defiant shake of her head, she sped up again and gathered herself as she eyed up the fallen tree.

"She's going to jump the tree!" Stella yelled. "I don't believe it!"

The riders sat and watched, utterly gobsmacked, as the buckskin sized up the formidable tree trunk in front of her. Like all of the Blackthorn Ponies, the mare couldn't have been any more than fourteen hands. The tree, meanwhile, was enormous. It reminded Issie of the cross-country fences in the Badminton Horse Trials – it was at least a metre and a half high and almost two metres wide.

As the little mare approached the fence Issie winced in fright. The mare was so tiny in comparison to this tree, she was bound to injure herself. There was a sickening moment when the buckskin launched herself into the air. And then Issie and the others watched in total amazement as she soared over it easily with nearly half a metre to spare, landing neatly on the other side without breaking her stride.

"I do not believe what I have just seen." Avery was stunned.

"Watch out! Here comes the next one!" Stella shouted.

The riders stood by helplessly as one pony after another took the enormous log in their stride, all of them leaping it with ease.

"Incredible!" Avery said.

"Can't we stop them, Tom?" Issie said. "They're all getting away."

"Maybe not all of them," Avery said, gesturing towards the back of the herd. "The mares with the foals. We can still stop them."

He was right. The foals were far too young and too tiny to make such an enormous jump. And their mothers would never leave them.

"Aidan!" Issie shouted. "The mares with the foals. Get the mares with the foals!"

"Everyone close in!" Avery shouted. The last of the herd had just hurdled the fallen log and only the two mares and their foals were left behind now. "Does anyone have a halter handy?"

"I do!" Stella said.

"Focus on the skewbald mare," Avery instructed her. "If you can catch the mother then her foal will stick with her."

"I'll take the grey!" Aidan called out. "I've got my halter too."

"Everyone else, keep your horses tight together. Close up behind Stella and Aidan and form a barricade," Avery instructed.

The riders moved in slowly as Stella and Aidan rode on just ahead of them. Stella had her halter in her hand as she moved closer to the skewbald mare. When she was within an arm's length she threw the rope of the halter over the pony's neck. The skewbald flinched, but she didn't fight back. She stood quivering as Stella held her firm with the rope, dismounted and quickly but gently eased the halter on to her. At the mare's feet the chestnut and white foal stood nervously by its mother.

"I've got her!" Stella sounded shocked. "I've got her!"

As Stella moved out of the way, leading the skewbald and her foal, Aidan urged Diablo up close to the little grey and reached one hand out to grab a handful of mane near her ears. Then he leant over and quickly pulled the halter on.

"Got this one too!" he shouted to the others. A cheer rose up from the riders.

"I don't believe it!" Stella said, positively beaming as she tied the rope from the skewbald's halter to her own saddle. "Look, Issie! I caught a wild horse! Me! I caught her! Isn't that so cool?"

Issie beamed back at her. "Let's get them home," she said.

As the riders led the Blackthorn mares back along the Coast Road towards the manor, they relived their adventure at Preacher's Cove. The little foals both trotted along briskly at their side, determined not to be separated.

While Stella and Kate continued to *oohh* and *ahh* over the foals, trying to decide which one was the absolute cutest, Issie fell back silently behind the rest of the ride.

"Something wrong?" Avery asked, pulling Dolomite up so that he could join her.

Issie nodded. "Oh, Tom. I know it's great that we caught the mares and the foals – but, well, there are another twenty-five horses still out there and really, the whole plan didn't work at all, did it?"

Avery looked down at Issie – Dolomite was so huge

that he towered over her. Issie could see that his face mirrored her own concerns.

"No. You're right. It didn't work. And even if we had managed to corral those horses I still don't think we would have been able to drive them all the way back to Hester's. It's a long way back to Blackthorn Manor. We could never muster and control all those horses over such a long distance…"

Avery looked at the mares and their foals trotting alongside Aidan and Stella. "Still, at least we saved these ones, Issie. That must count for something."

They were almost at the manor now and as they trotted down the limestone driveway one of the Blackthorn mares, the little skewbald, let out a loud whinny. Her cry was immediately returned by an even louder call – the shrill, penetrating cry of a stallion calling for his mares.

"That's Destiny!" Issie said. "He must know that his mares are here."

When they heard the stallion's cry both the mares whinnied back in return. Their paces quickened as they set off down the driveway towards the stallion.

"Hey!" Stella yelped as the skewbald pulled hard on the lead rope, dragging her along. "Well, I guess it's a family reunion!" she giggled when she saw the stallion snorting and pacing the fence-line with excitement at the mares' arrival.

"You're back!" Hester grinned, emerging from the stables to greet them all. "I had got the stables ready for thirty, but four is a good start! Pop these mums and their little ones into the paddock next to Destiny, will you, Aidan?" she said. "Is this all you managed to bring home with you?"

"I'm afraid so," Stella said as she helped Aidan let the skewbald and her foal loose.

"Those foals don't look like Blackthorn ponies to me," Hester said, running her eyes over the two young colts cantering about on wobbly limbs, following their mums. "Look at those long legs! They both seem to have Destiny's lovely elevated paces too. Even that darling little skewbald lad seems to take after his dad…"

"Do you think Destiny is their sire?" Issie asked her aunt.

"I'd say so." Hester smiled. "Avignon's grandfoals. I'm quite sure of it."

As the riders watched, the pretty grey mare trotted up to the rails and poked her head over to greet Destiny. The stallion ran straight up to her and as their noses touched he gave a squeal, rearing up and racing impatiently up and down his side of the fence-line with the mare running alongside him on the other side.

"He wants to be with them. You can't keep a family apart," Hester said as they watched the stallion snorting his way along the fence-line.

"That's it!" Avery said.

"What? What's it?" Issie looked at her instructor

"That's our answer," Avery said.

"Umm… what was our question again?" Issie was confused.

"I think I've come up with a way to capture the rest of the wild ponies and bring them back to Blackthorn Manor." He turned to Issie now. "Issie, quick as you can – put Blaze away, and then ask Stella to do us a favour and groom her and bed her down for you. You won't have time for that now. I need you to meet me in the round pen. And bring your saddle and bridle and helmet. There's a girl – off you go!"

Issie stood rooted to the spot. "I don't understand, Tom. Why do I need my gear if I'm putting Blaze away for the night. Who am I going to be riding?"

Avery turned to her. "Isadora, I'm sorry, I'm not explaining myself clearly but time is of the essence so you'll have to trust me. I've come up with a way for us to lead the wild ponies home. And you and Destiny are the key."

Issie was still confused. "I'm sorry, Tom, I still don't understand…" she began.

"You saw how the mares reacted when they saw Destiny," Avery said. "Those ponies are a family. And we have the head of the family right here. They will follow him anywhere… you can lead them anywhere…"

"You mean, you want me to ride Destiny?" Issie was shocked.

Avery nodded. "He trusts you. I don't think any other rider would stand a chance, but with you riding him, maybe we can be ready in time. We still have the rest of the afternoon. The cull isn't until tomorrow…"

"You mean you want me to break Destiny in? In just one day?"

"Well, not so much a day as an afternoon," Avery said, looking at his watch. "Anyway, if it could be done and it was our only chance, wouldn't you say that we had to give it a go? Issie? What do you say?"

Issie looked across at her Aunt. "Aunty Hess?"

Hester nodded. "Tom is right, Issie. Destiny is our link to the wild herd. He trusts you. Plus you'll be light on his back; Destiny has never had a rider before."

Hester paused. "It has to be your choice. Your mother would kill me if she thought I was behind something like this. She'll probably kill me anyway. But I've watched you ride and I think you can do it. The question is, do you think you can do it?"

Issie looked at the big, black stallion. He was still pacing the fence-line and whinnying across the paddocks at his mares. The rest of his herd were still out there somewhere and tomorrow they would be killed in the cull.

"I'll ask Stella to put Blaze away for me," Issie said. "I'll get my gear and be right back!" And then she was off and running to the stables. Avery was right. There was no time to lose. Destiny was waiting for her.

CHAPTER 13

Issie's tummy churned with nerves as she walked into the round pen. She put her saddle and bridle down on the sawdust and looked around her. The last time she had been here, Aidan had tried to teach her how to trick-jump with Blaze and she had lost her nerve. If she wasn't brave enough to leap from Blaze's back on to Paris that day, there was no way she would ever be brave enough to ride Destiny. Maybe she should just give up right now – tell Avery that she couldn't do it. He would understand…

"Feeling nervous?" Avery's voice startled her.

"Uh-huh," Issie said.

"I need you to get rid of your doubts right now, Isadora," Avery said. "It's very important that you are confident, that you believe you can do this. A horse will always sense your fear. And there is no room for mistakes in this arena. It's vital that you feel strong and in control when Destiny comes in here."

"But, Tom, I'm not sure I can do this. He's a wild stallion and we don't have enough time…"

"Isadora, we have plenty of time. And you," he smiled at her, "you have more than enough courage."

"Now," Avery continued, "I'm going to explain the ropes to you before Aidan brings Destiny in."

"But, Tom," Issie interrupted him, "you'll be in there with me… won't you?"

Avery shook his head. "I can't come into the ring with you – this is something you need to do alone, Issie. You must make a bond with this horse."

"That's crazy!" Issie said. "I don't know how to break in a wild horse."

"You've been in my natural horsemanship classes before, haven't you? Well consider this your final lesson," Avery said. He pointed to the tiered seats that ran around the edge of the round pen. "I'll be watching you and calling instructions to you. Just do exactly as I tell you." Avery looked at her. "Now, can you do this?"

Issie took a deep breath. "OK, I mean yes, Tom, absolutely. I'm ready – let's do it."

As Avery explained how the training session would work, Issie sat listening intently. She was trying very hard to concentrate on absolutely everything that Avery was telling her, but there was so much to learn.

"Don't worry," Avery said as he left her alone in the arena. "I promise you, in less than an hour we're going to have you up on Destiny's back and riding him."

Avery left the round pen and Aidan came in leading Destiny. The black stallion was clearly spooked by his new surroundings. As Aidan led him past Issie the big, black horse shied at his own shadow, rearing up and jerking the lead rope almost out of Aidan's hand. "Easy boy," Aidan said. Issie could see the horse's nostrils quivering and there was sweat on his flanks.

He's afraid too, Issie realised, and at that moment her nerves completely vanished. If Destiny was scared, then it was up to her to be brave enough for both of them.

"You can let Destiny loose now," Avery called down to Aidan. Aidan nodded. He unclipped the lead rope from the halter. It took a moment for Destiny to realise that he was now free, and then he shook his head defiantly and cantered off to stand on the far side of the round pen, as far away as he could get from Issie and Aidan.

Aidan walked over to Issie and handed her the lead rope.

"Are you going to be OK in here by yourself?" he asked her.

"Uh-huh," she said. "I think so."

Aidan smiled. "I'm right outside that door if you need me." And with that, he headed back across the sawdust floor and out of the arena – shutting the door behind him, leaving Issie alone with the stallion.

"Right. We need to move fast here, Issie," Avery said. "Let's get started."

Issie nodded. Then she turned to face the stallion, her shoulders square to him, her gaze directly meeting his eyes. For a moment the horse looked back at her, holding her stare and challenging her.

"Use the rope now, Issie," Avery commanded from above.

Issie looked down at the long lead rope in her hand. She swung it around like a lasso and then let it fly. The rope flicked out and landed uselessly on the sawdust in front of her. Issie felt herself getting flustered – Aidan and Avery were watching from the seats above and she had no idea what she was doing.

"Don't worry about it. Try again," Avery said. "It will take you a few throws to get used to the weight of the rope."

Issie pulled the rope back, looping it loose in her hand and then threw it again. This time the rope flew out perfectly, tapping Destiny lightly across the rump. Destiny snorted with surprise and began to trot around the perimeter of the round pen. The rope fell away behind the stallion and Issie pulled it towards her, looping it back in her hands.

"That's it. Excellent. And again," Avery called to her.

Issie flicked the rope again and this time the stallion broke into a canter.

"Very good!" Avery said. "Those taps with the rope will keep him moving. Don't let him stop. We're going to keep him running for a while and pretty soon he'll get tired of going around this pen and he'll want to stop running. He's going to want to come to you instead, which means he's becoming submissive and acknowledging you as the 'alpha' horse, the boss of the herd. All you need to do now is keep him moving and look for the signs that I told you about."

Issie nodded at Avery's words but she didn't dare to take her eyes off the black horse and look up at her instructor. Avery had told her that she must never look away from Destiny, not even for a moment.

Destiny was cantering gracefully, his head held high, his nostrils flared. Issie found it impossible to believe that this proud, powerful, wild stallion would ever allow her to become the boss. Hadn't he always been the boss of his herd? She flicked the long rope at Destiny again to keep the horse cantering, waiting and watching like Avery had told her to, looking for a sign.

"There!" Avery called over the edge of the arena. "Do you see that, Issie?"

"Ummm, what?" Issie called up.

"He's listening to you. His ears are swivelling towards you, his head is turning towards you. He's paying attention now," Avery said excitedly. "In a moment he's going to make more signals – he'll lick his lips and lower his head. This is his way of saying, 'I accept that you are in charge – please let me stop running now'."

As Avery said this the black horse began to do exactly that. He lowered his head and licked his lips.

"You've got him!" Avery said. "OK, Issie, now look down at the ground and don't make eye contact. Look straight down at the ground. Do it now."

Issie did as Avery instructed. Almost immediately Destiny stopped running. Issie stayed perfectly still. The stallion took a step towards her and then another. He stretched out his nose to sniff at her. He took another step. He was so close to Issie that he was almost touching her.

"Don't make eye contact – just put your hand out, give him a pat," Avery said. The stallion didn't flinch as she reached out and stroked his face and neck. He even stood patient and relaxed as Issie stroked along his shoulders and rump. He seemed to be enjoying her touch.

"That's right, touch him along his back – that's where horses like to groom each other – he's letting you in now, you're the alpha." Avery's voice was calm and firm as he spoke to her. "Now turn away from him, Issie. Turn your back on him and walk away now," Avery told her.

Issie felt herself stiffen at this. Did she really have to turn her back on this wild horse? What if Destiny attacked her?

"It's OK," Avery said softly. "You can do it. He won't hurt you."

Issie kept her eyes down on the ground and turned her back on Destiny. She began to walk away, and as she walked she could hear the horse right there behind her.

"Don't look back," Avery said firmly.

"Tom! What's going on? Is he following me?" she hissed.

Avery laughed. "That's right. You're the alpha now. Go ahead and take him for a walk. He'll follow you."

Issie giggled and began to walk around the arena with Destiny following along right behind her like a puppy dog on a leash – except there was no leash. The horse was right there next to her, his nose nudging against her sleeve.

"This is cool!" Issie smiled up at Avery as she walked a whole circle around the arena with Destiny following at her side.

"OK, alpha girl. You can put the saddle and bridle on him now," Avery said. "It looks like you've got yourself a new partner."

Issie couldn't believe how easy it had been to win Destiny over. But the thrill of becoming the "alpha" quickly faded when she strapped the saddle on and Destiny began to buck uncontrollably.

"It's fine, let him buck," Avery reassured her. "He's never worn a saddle before. Just let him get it out of his system and he'll come back to you."

Avery was right. Destiny quickly calmed down and let Issie put on a bridle too.

"OK, Aidan, you can come back in now," Avery called. Aidan stepped into the arena. "Give Issie a leg up," Avery instructed.

"What?" Issie couldn't believe it. "But I've only just put the saddle on! It's been less than an hour! You can't break a horse in this fast!"

"Isadora. Do you trust me?" Avery said.

"Uh-huh," Issie replied.

"Then get on. He's ready. You'll be fine. Remember, you're the alpha."

"I'm the alpha, I'm the alpha," Issie chanted over and over under her breath as she put her knee in Aidan's cupped hand and sprang lightly into the saddle. Issie looked down. She had never been this high up on a horse before. Destiny was much bigger than either Blaze or Mystic. He was nearly sixteen hands. It felt like a million miles up in the air. Issie slipped her feet into the stirrups and grasped the reins in her hands. Beneath her she felt Destiny tremble, his muscles tensed as if he were ready to bolt.

"Do you want me to keep holding him?" Aidan asked. He had both hands firmly on Destiny's reins.

Issie shook her head. "No, Aidan. Let him go. It's the only way." She took a deep breath, braced her feet against the stirrups and held on.

As Destiny took a step and felt the weight of the rider on his back he gave a little half-buck. Issie hung on, her hands gripping tightly now to the front of the saddle. Destiny snorted, lowered his head and bucked again. It was a big buck this time and she felt herself lifting up and crashing back down into the saddle, but she didn't fall off.

"He's OK. He's just getting used to you," Avery said calmly. "Put your legs on him and ask him to move forward."

Issie took a deep breath and did as Avery asked. Nothing. Destiny held his ground against her, refusing to move. Frustrated, Issie gave the big, black horse a swift kick. "Get-up!" she demanded, growling under her breath nervously.

As Issie's heels dug into his sides Destiny gave a snort of defiance and reared straight up in the air and Issie, who hadn't been expecting it, flung herself at his neck, grasping desperately at his mane to hang on.

"Stop it!" she growled as the stallion thrashed the air with his hooves. By the time Destiny plunged back down again, Issie was white and shaking like a leaf.

"Are you OK?" Avery called to her.

"I think so," Issie said. "He was fine one minute and then I kicked him and he just went up without any warning at all."

"This is your first time on a stallion, isn't it, Issie?" Avery asked.

Issie nodded.

"In the past you've ridden geldings and mares," Avery continued. "A gelding, of course, is a castrated horse, which means he's pretty docile by nature. You can get as bossy as you like with a gelding. They're easygoing and they don't mind if you push them around and tell them what to do. Mares can be temperamental, but if you ask a mare like Blaze nicely enough then she'll do pretty much anything, yes?"

Issie nodded at this.

"Stallions are different," Avery said. "They're used to being in charge. They're strong-willed and they don't take orders." Avery looked serious. "You need to treat them with the utmost respect. If you try and force a stallion against his will like you did just then he'll turn against you, Issie. You must convince a stallion that he wants to work for you. Never, ever fight him – you won't win that way."

Issie nodded.

"OK," Avery said, "I think he's calmed down now. Talk to him, Issie. Ask him to move forward and take a lap around the arena…That's good! See how his ears are swivelling? He's listening. Now ask him to canter."

When Issie put her legs on the big, black horse he objected a little, but Issie didn't lose her cool. She softened her hands, whispered softly to the stallion and tried again. Destiny gave a snort, arched his neck, and instead of battling her, he flung his right leg out into a perfect smooth canter transition.

"Excellent, excellent. Now you're talking!" Avery said. "This is good progress. Are you ready to ask him for more? Here's where the lesson really begins…"

Over the next two hours Issie slowly gained Destiny's confidence. They began moving around the arena in perfect harmony, the stallion cantering on her command and then halting again with the lightest touch of the reins.

"Now ask him to turn left, now right…" Avery called to her from the seats up above the arena. "Good, good, excellent! That's enough for today. You can get off now – and take his saddle and bridle off too. We're done."

There was a clapping noise from the other side of the arena and Issie looked up to see Stella, Kate, Dan and Ben.

"That was amazing!" Stella said. "I totally held my breath when you were getting on him! And then when he reared up, I was sure you were going to fall off!"

Issie grinned up at her friends in the seats above her. "Have you guys been there the whole time?"

"Pretty much the whole time," Kate said. "Avery said we could watch as long as we didn't disturb you."

"Well, you're disturbing her now," Avery grumped at the girls. "Isadora, don't dawdle. You need to put Destiny away for the night."

Avery turned to the other riders who were now leaning over the sides of the round pen watching. "If you lot have all fed your horses then you can head back up to the house and help Hester. She's getting dinner ready. There'll be plenty of time for chit-chat when the food is on the table."

Everyone was so desperately hungry after the day's adventures that they wolfed down their meals before beginning to talk about the breaking-in of Destiny.

"I still can't believe I actually rode him!" Issie said, shaking her head.

"You two made great progress today," Avery agreed. "But I wish we had another day up our sleeves. We don't know how Destiny will behave outside the round pen in the open countryside, or what will happen when he meets the wild herd again."

Issie nodded. She had suddenly lost her appetite – and it wasn't because she had already eaten two helpings of roast chicken. Avery was right. It was easy to ride Destiny in the round pen. The real test would be riding him outside where there were no fences to stop him.

Although she guessed they would find out soon enough.

"I was wondering," Stella said as she heaped a third helping on to her plate, "do we have a plan yet? I mean, I know Issie is going to ride Destiny and he'll hopefully lead the herd. But is that it?"

Avery cocked an eyebrow at Stella. "You're right, of course, Stella. I think we all agree that a plan is needed." Avery paused. "And luckily for us, Aidan has one. A rather good one actually. We should talk about it now, since we'll need to leave early in the morning again. So gather round everyone. Here's what we're going to do…"

As Aunt Hester brought out dessert Avery and Aidan explained the plan to the others. There was much nodding and frowning as the riders talked it over. Then they began to use whatever was on the table – dessert spoons, pudding bowls and cream jugs – to mark out a strategy map so they could figure out the details.

"Just pretend I'm the sugar spoon…" Stella shouted out at one point, moving the spoon across the table. "What about if I go over here by the teapot…"

"No! No!" Kate said to her. "You need to be back here on the place mat with the rest of the dessert spoons…"

They carried on like this for quite some time until they all felt certain that the plan would work. Then, when Hester suggested they should all go to bed, ready for an early start, no one argued. As the riders headed for their rooms, there was a mood of optimism in the manor.

"Do you really think we can pull this off?" Issie asked Tom as she stood up from the kitchen table.

Avery looked down at the dishes sprawled about in front of him. "I don't think ponies are quite as easy to manoeuvre as teaspoons," he said, "but yes, yes, Issie, I think we have a very good chance indeed." He smiled at her. "Now, get some sleep. Tomorrow is a big day. I can't have my alpha horse exhausted before we even begin."

Issie smiled and climbed the stairs to her room. She washed her face, brushed her teeth and put on her pyjamas before climbing beneath the soft cotton sheets of the enormous four-poster bed. Then she lay there silently, taking one last, long look at the portrait of Avignon above her fireplace before she turned out the light.

CHAPTER 14

The crunch of car tyres on the limestone driveway woke Issie up. She could hear car doors slamming and the sounds of whispered conversations just outside the front door of the manor.

This was ridiculous! She knew Avery wanted to get an early start, but it wasn't even light outside. She didn't want to get up yet; she was still half asleep.

Issie sat bolt upright in bed. That wasn't Tom's voice she could hear downstairs. She listened again and felt a sudden chill as she realised who it was.

Flinging herself out of bed and wrapping a dressing gown quickly around her, Issie sprinted across the landing and down the stairs. She flew out the front door and crashed straight into Cameron, making him drop his clipboard.

"Good Morning," the ranger said stiffly as he bent down and picked his paperwork up.

"What are you doing here?" Issie blurted out. "It's not even light yet!"

"We're making an early start. My men are assembling here at the manor. We'll be out of your hair shortly."

"What do you mean you're meeting here?" Issie demanded.

"Your aunt agreed to it," Cameron shrugged, "take it up with her." He turned away and scribbled something down on his clipboard, making it clear that the conversation was over as far as he was concerned.

"Aunty Hess! Aunty Hess!" Issie raced frantically through the house.

"I'm out here!" Hester called from the back porch.

Issie found Hester out by the boot rack pulling a single pink Hunter wellington on to her foot, the one that didn't have a cast on it.

"Isadora, dear. Why are you still in your pyjamas? We need to get a move on, you know!" Hester said.

"Aunty Hess, did you tell Cameron that his men could all meet here before they began the cull?" Issie panted. She'd been hunting the whole manor for her aunt and she was clean out of breath.

"Yes, dear. I did," Hester said matter-of-factly.

"Aunty Hess! How could you? Why would you help them?" Issie was furious.

"Help them? I'm doing nothing of the kind. I just wanted to have one more chance to get them together and reason with them about this whole cull business," Hester said. "Now, where is Cameron – the front porch? Ask him to come into the kitchen, will you? I'll make us all some tea."

When Issie went back to the front of the house to find the ranger she saw another three cars had arrived in the driveway. Five men, all dressed in the same uniform as Cameron, were now gathered in conversation on the front porch. All of them were carrying guns.

"Aunt Hester would like to talk to you," Issie told Cameron. "She's made a pot of tea if you'd like to come in."

The ranger nodded, then he turned to his men. "Wait here for me. We'll set off as soon as it's light. This won't take long." And with that he followed Issie inside.

"Ah, Cameron!" Hester greeted the ranger. "Cup of tea?"

"Thanks, Hester," he replied gruffly, sitting down at the kitchen table.

"Cameron," Hester continued, "I know it's going to seem like a dreadful waste of time for you, now that you've got your men out so bright and early, but the thing is, we're going to bring the rest of the herd in today. It's very good news actually – we've come up with a way to find homes for them all. My niece's riding instructor is very well connected with the International League for the Protection of Horses and he's kindly going to help us find new owners for all the Blackthorn Ponies."

Hester sat down opposite Cameron and poured the tea before continuing, "We had planned to have the herd back here at the farm already, but we've had a few setbacks. Still, we're going to bring all the horses in today. So you needn't bother with the cull. If you want to go out now and tell your men they can go home, that would be lovely…" Hester paused. "Naturally they're welcome to come in and have a cup of tea before they go home. I've put the jug back on and—"

Cameron shook his head. "I'm sorry, Hester. I can't do that."

"Whatever do you mean?" Hester said. "If they'd

prefer coffee, of course, I can make a pot—"

"No, Hester. I mean, I can't call the cull off. It's going ahead as planned. You've already delayed us so many times now. We've had petitions and Conservation Trust meetings and lawyers meetings. Then your niece tries to sidetrack us with all this talk of a Grimalkin – some mythical creature that my men have been wasting their time over…"

Issie couldn't believe this. "I didn't make it up! The Grimalkin is real…" she began. But Cameron hushed her with a sullen glare and continued.

"So we don't find any trace of this 'Grimalkin'. And then you tell us you can catch the horses. You promised you'd catch the herd and bring them home to your farm if we just gave you more time. Friday was the deadline and today is Friday. There's a limit Hester and you've reached it. My men are here to do their job. None of us wanted this cull to happen, but it is going to happen. You can't stop it now; it's too late. We're taking our guns and we're going out there. I'm sorry, but it's got to be done."

Hester stared at the ranger. "Cameron. I'm asking you. As a friend. Please – give us just a little more time. What difference will one more day make? It means nothing to you but it may save these horses' lives. Isn't there anything you can do?"

Cameron looked down at the mug of tea in front of him and sat in silence for a moment. Then he looked up at Hester. "I can't give you the day," he said with a glint in his eye, "but I can give you a couple of hours to get a head start."

He turned to look at Issie. "I think my men could do with a big, hearty breakfast before we head out there to look for the herd. Issie, if your aunt wouldn't mind serving us up some farm eggs and bacon, and perhaps doing us a few of her famous griddle scones... and then after that we'll spend some time consulting our maps and doing a bit of a rifle check... well, it could take us a couple of hours before we're ready to set off."

He looked at his watch. "It's six a.m. now – all that should keep us busy until about eight a.m..."

"Thank you, Cameron," Hester said.

"Yes, thanks," Issie said.

"Are you still here?" Cameron looked sternly at Issie. "I thought you would have been out there saddling up your horses by now. You don't have that much time."

"I'm gone," Issie said as she raced for the door.

Dust clouds billowed up as the horse truck belted along the Coast Road heading for Preacher's Cove. Sitting in the front seat, Issie looked at the speedometer and then checked her watch. It was nearly seven a.m. "Come on, Aidan!"

"I'm driving as fast as I can. We'll be there in less than five minutes," Aidan snapped back at her.

Issie and her friends had made the most of the ranger's two-hour head start. Instead of setting out on horseback for the cove as the ranger had assumed they would, they had loaded their horses into the truck.

All the horses were on board except Dolomite. Since Issie was riding Destiny it had been decided that Stella would ride Blaze and Avery would ride Paris. "We need Blaze's speed and agility; it will come in handy for the muster," Avery reasoned. "Besides, it will keep Destiny happy in the horse truck if Blaze is at his side."

Issie looked back now through the window of the truck cab. She could see Blaze and Destiny standing side by side in their partitions, the stallion craning his neck around to get closer to the chestnut mare.

"How many of the Blackthorn Ponies do you think you can fit in here?" Issie asked.

"It's big enough to take seven horses the size of

Dolomite, so I dunno, about fifteen if we're lucky," Aidan said.

Issie looked worried. "It's not enough, Aidan," she sighed. "That still leaves maybe ten horses that won't make it on to the truck."

"We can herd the stragglers home," Aidan said. "There's six of us on horseback. We should be able to manage the ones who are left behind."

When they reached Preacher's Cove Aidan parked the horse truck at the top of the hill.

"Let's get them off quickly everyone," Avery said. Issie moved swiftly inside as soon as the ramp was lowered, hurrying to untie Destiny's ropes. "Easy, Destiny, good boy," she murmured. The black stallion was in surprisingly good shape after the journey. He seemed to take the truck ride in his stride.

"Good lad, Destiny. Come on, we're here now…" Issie said. Destiny picked his hooves up neatly and precisely as he marched down the ramp of the truck. At the end of the ramp the black horse lifted his head high and scanned the horizon. His nostrils were flared wide as he sniffed the air.

"Do you think he'll be able to find his herd?" Issie asked Aidan.

"His instincts are strong. He'll find them," Aidan said. "Let him go wherever he wants. All you have to do is get on him and hang on."

Is that all I have to do? Issie thought to herself. Aidan made it sound so easy. Had he forgotten that this was a wild stallion? Just yesterday she had ridden Destiny for the very first time. Now here she was, taking him out alone on to the open plains to reunite him with his herd.

"I'd better go saddle him up then," Issie said.

"Do you want help?" Aidan asked.

Issie shook her head. "It's better if I do this alone. You go and help the others."

Issie went to the truck and grabbed her saddle. Then she returned to Destiny's side. The stallion was shifting about nervously, his nose still high in the air. Was it the scent of his herd that had captured his attention? Issie wondered.

She moved very deliberately and slowly as she put the saddle on Destiny's back and did up the girth. The horse didn't flinch as the strap tightened around his belly. "Good lad," Issie breathed softly. She drew the bridle up gently over his face now and quickly did up the straps, then pulled on her helmet and fastened her chin strap. She checked the girth one last time.

"All ready?" Tom Avery appeared at her side. "Do you want a leg up?"

"Uh-huh, I guess so," Issie said.

Avery took Destiny's reins in one hand and offered the other hand to Issie for a leg up. She put her knee in Avery's hand and with a quick bounce she leapt up into the saddle. Avery was still holding the reins. He seemed reluctant to let go.

"When you find the herd, let him take control," Avery instructed. "He'll do what comes naturally to him. Then all you need to do is guide him back towards the cove. Get the herd to follow you down to the sea and then we'll do the rest."

Issie nodded. She straightened the peak on her helmet and took up the reins. She noticed that her hands were trembling a little.

Avery noticed too. "You know, Issie, you don't have to do this," he said gently.

"I know. I'm not scared, Tom, honest," she replied.

"Remember," Avery said, "you're the alpha."

"I'm the alpha." Issie smiled at him. Then she wheeled the stallion around to face the road.

"I'll see you soon. Be ready for me," Issie called back. And with that, she clucked the stallion into a canter, riding him swiftly up and over the crest of the hill, along the Coast Road that would lead her to Lake Deepwater.

As they cantered along the Coast Road Issie steeled her nerve and let the reins go slack so that the big, black horse was in control. *Give him his head*, she thought, *let him find his own way. He will lead me to the herd.*

Destiny immediately sensed his freedom and broke into a gallop. Issie wrapped her hands tight in his mane and clung on.

As the stallion veered off the Coast Road and began to skilfully pick his way across the rocky terrain at full gallop Issie fought the urge to snatch back the reins and slow him down. Destiny was going far too fast. *If he stops suddenly*, Issie thought, *I'll go flying over his head.*

At that very moment Destiny gave a sudden lurch to the left to avoid a large rock and Issie felt herself sliding uncontrollably to one side. For a moment she was sure she was going to fall. But she managed to hang on to the hank of mane that she had tangled in her hands and in a couple of strides she had righted herself again.

Hang on, she thought to herself. *No matter what, you have to hang on...*

Destiny slowed down to a canter as he rose up over the brow of a hill. He let out a loud, vigorous whinny as he surveyed the valley below. Issie scanned the fields in front of her but there was nothing to see except green pasture and a few blackthorn trees. Destiny whinnied again. Still nothing. The stallion stood alert, his ears pricked forward. He was listening, waiting. And then, from out of nowhere, came the whinny of a horse returning his call. Issie's heart raced. He had found the herd.

Issie was left behind in the saddle as Destiny lunged forward and began galloping headlong down the hill. From the other direction she heard the low thunder of hoofbeats as the herd approached.

When Issie had first met the Blackthorn Ponies they seemed to be one big faceless herd, but now, she realised, she was beginning to recognise each of them as distinct individuals. They were all so wild, so alive. Issie felt herself choking back her anger at the rangers and their stupid cull. How could anyone ever think of hurting these beautiful horses?

The herd slowed down to a trot as the stallion reached them. Issie had been worried that they would scatter when they saw her on Destiny's back, but the ponies seemed not to notice or care about her.

The stallion cantered a wide circle around the herd, establishing his territory. Then he moved closer, nipping and lunging at his mares to snap them into line, asserting his authority over the other horses. The buckskin mare wasn't easily subdued. She lashed out with her hind legs as he nipped at her and Issie had to hang on once again as Destiny swerved to avoid her flying hooves.

When the stallion seemed satisfied that his herd were all under control he began to move them back up the hill. Issie held on tight to his mane, resisting the temptation to touch the reins. Destiny was heading back towards the cove, exactly where they needed to go, and the ponies were following him. All she had to do was hang on.

When they reached the hill at the top of the valley she expected Destiny to trot on straight ahead, back down to the Coast Road and the cove. But the black horse seemed to suddenly change his mind. He broke into a canter, altered his direction and turned along the ridge in completely the wrong direction.

"Destiny, NO!" Issie pulled hard on the right rein to turn the stallion around. As soon as she had done it, she realised her mistake. *Never, ever fight him.* She remembered Tom Avery's words. *You won't win that way.*

As he felt the jarring of the metal bit pulling harshly in his mouth Destiny responded by fighting back. He reared up, his front legs thrashing the air in front of him. Then, as he came back down with Issie still on his back, he gave an almighty buck.

Issie had fallen off her horse loads of times, but this fall was different. Destiny's buck sent her flying up in the air in a dramatic arc. It all happened so fast there was nothing she could do to soften the fall. She hit the ground with such force, she immediately felt the wind being knocked out of her. Breathless and shocked Issie tried to push herself up on her elbows, coughing and heaving as her lungs struggled desperately for air. As she propped herself up on her arms she felt a shooting pain down her left arm and the thought flashed through her head that her wrist must be broken.

She stayed there on the ground a bit longer. She was too dizzy to stand up; the ground and the sky were spinning around her. What had just happened? Where was Destiny?

The nicker of a horse brought her back to reality. She took a deep breath and pulled herself together. She needed to stand up and look for her horse. Issie forced herself to her feet. The sun on the horizon was blinding her now but she could make out the shape of a horse. He was coming towards her.

"Destiny?" Issie croaked. And then there he was in front of her. Not a big, black stallion at all, but a little grey gelding. Weak and exhausted from her fall, Issie fell forward and wrapped her arms around the horse's neck, hugging him tightly, her face buried in his mane. It was Mystic.

CHAPTER 15

What a complete disaster! Right now Avery and the others would be waiting at the cove for Issie to return, leading the herd back to them. They had no way of knowing Destiny was gone and there was no sign of the wild ponies. The clock was ticking. The rangers would be here soon, tracking down the herd to begin their cull. She had to do something – and fast!

Issie scanned the horizon desperately. Then she turned to the little grey gelding. "Mystic! You found them before – you can do it again. We've got to get those horses back!"

She looked around for somewhere to mount up and spied a fallen tree just a few metres away. If she climbed up on that log, it would be easy to make a leap on to the little grey's back. Issie put a hand out to grasp Mystic's silvery mane, and let out a sudden squeal, doubling over in pain. She had forgotten about her injured wrist. She gave her fingers one more tentative wiggle and winced as the pain shot up her arm. She was pretty sure it wasn't broken but it was still really sore. She couldn't ride like this.

Issie felt tears of anger and frustration welling up. She had to get on Mystic's back if she was to stand any chance at all of finding the Blackthorn Ponies. But how could she do it with an injured wrist?

Calm down, she told herself sternly, *calm down and think, Issie*. She paused for a moment and then, very carefully so as not to hurt her wrist, she pulled off her jacket. It was one of those stretch velour tracksuit jackets, pale blue with white stripes. She took it and knotted one sleeve around the elbow of her injured arm, checking that it was firm but not too tight. Then she took the other sleeve and used her teeth once more to tie a knot with the end of the sleeve around her sore wrist. With the sleeves secured at her elbow and her wrist she pulled the rest of the jacket up and over her head, wriggling and squirming her head through so that the jacket was now strung over her shoulder with the sleeves stretched taut, holding her arm in a makeshift sling.

"If I can't use that arm, I'm just going to have to keep it out of the way," she said to Mystic. Grabbing a hank of his mane with her right hand she led the horse over to the log, trying to protect her injured wrist as she vaulted lightly on to his back. Steadying herself, she wrapped her good hand tightly in Mystic's mane. *As long as I can hold on and ride with just one hand,* Issie thought…

"Let's go, Mystic." She gave the grey gelding a light tap with her heels to let him know she was ready. "Go find them for me." The little grey immediately set off at a fast canter, following the trail of the Blackthorn herd.

Issie had ridden Mystic bareback many times before, but one-handed bareback added a whole new challenge. As the little pony galloped on she tried to keep her balance by staying low and gripping with her legs. She sat tight and didn't even try to guide him; Mystic seemed to know exactly where he was going.

"Oh, where are they, Mystic?" Issie said. They had to find the ponies fast. It must have been nearly two hours since Issie had left the farm. The rangers would be loading up their four-wheel-drives right now and heading this way.

Thankfully it didn't take Mystic long to track down

the herd. When the grey gelding galloped up to a plateau overlooking the Coast Road, Issie let out a cry of relief. There they were! Destiny and the ponies – and not more than a hundred metres away.

The black stallion still had his saddle and bridle on and he was grazing happily alongside the buckskin mare. When he saw Mystic he raised his head and stood, alert and watchful, as if deciding whether to spur his herd into action and run again.

Issie and Mystic froze too and Issie could feel her heart racing as she realised what she was about to do. Her plan was dangerous and she knew it. She wasn't in the best shape to take on a stallion – the throbbing pain in her arm reminded her of that.

She looked at the ponies. She had to act fast. This was her last chance – and their last chance too.

"Come on, Mystic!" she said decisively.

Mystic moved swiftly into a gallop as Issie turned the little grey around in a wide circle and then began bearing down on the black stallion, approaching him from the rear.

Destiny had been waiting, watching them and deciding what he would do next. Now, as Issie and Mystic got closer, the black horse began to run. Destiny had a bigger stride than Mystic. He should have been able to outrun the little grey gelding. But Mystic had the element of surprise on his side. The little pony had already gathered speed and was now in full gallop. He had gained too much ground for the stallion to get away from him that easily. Mystic swiftly caught up to the big, black horse. Issie could feel him grunting and heaving with the effort of keeping pace with the stallion. The two horses were racing now, and Mystic was giving his all to stay neck-and-neck alongside Destiny.

Galloping hard, Mystic moved closer and closer to the black stallion. When the horses were matching each other stride for stride, Issie, who had been leaning low over Mystic's neck, suddenly sat up straight. She untangled her hands from Mystic's mane and then let go so that she was riding with no hands at all, her right arm held outstretched, her left hand tucked into the sling. Only her natural balance now kept her on Mystic's back.

Issie thought back to that day in the round pen when Aidan had tried to teach her the Flying Angel. She hadn't been able to do it then. Could she really do it now? There was no round pen out here on the open plains. She was racing at a wild gallop against an unpredictable stallion, and she had an injured arm. Even if she made the leap, would she be able to hang on?

Issie took a deep breath. There was only one way to find out.

"Now, Mystic!" she shouted at the pony. The grey gelding lengthened his stride and got even closer to the black stallion so that the two horses were almost brushing up against one another. Issie looked over at Destiny, then her eyes lowered to the ground below her. She saw the hooves thrashing beneath her and for a moment she felt sick. She couldn't do this!

Yes, you can, she told herself firmly. *Just don't look down. In fact, don't look at anything!* Issie turned in the saddle to face Destiny. She put out her hands and began the countdown. Ah-one, ah-two, ah-three. She shut her eyes and screwed them tight. Everything went black and she held her breath and took a flying leap.

There was a split second as she left Mystic's back when she felt absolutely nothing underneath her except for a rush of air and the thunder of hooves dragging her down. Then she felt her right hand grasp the leather of Destiny's saddle. She opened her eyes and began pulling herself up, dragging herself on to the black horse. Forgetting about the pain in her arm she clung on desperately with both hands, hooking her left foot into the stirrup and swinging her right foot high over the back of the saddle. Her hands hurried to find the reins. There they were! She took them up very gently so she wouldn't spook Destiny. She wasn't making that mistake again. Slowly, carefully, she pulled the black stallion to a canter and then slowed to a trot.

It took her moment to realise that she had done it. And then there she was. She was back on Destiny! The black horse was hers again.

Issie steadied the stallion to a halt and looked around. Mystic was nowhere to be seen, but the Blackthorn Ponies were still with her. They had followed Destiny when he ran and now they stood there, all of them with their ears pricked and their expressions alert, watching the black stallion, waiting for him to decide what they would do next.

"Easy, Destiny," Issie spoke softly to the big, black horse. "We need them to follow us. You have to lead them. Do you think you can do it?"

Did the stallion understand her? Did he know that she was trying to save his herd? Issie didn't know, but Destiny did seem to listen to her voice this time as she coaxed him on. Issie circled wide around the herd, slowly edging Destiny closer towards them, driving the ponies forward.

Issie was pretty sure they were heading in the right direction. Still, when they rounded the corner and she saw the Coast Road and Preacher's Cove ahead of them her heart soared. They were almost there! She pushed Destiny on to quicken his pace now, overtaking the herd and sweeping around to the right, driving them down the road towards the sea.

"Not much further, Destiny," she breathed to the stallion. "We're almost there…" They were coming up to the brow of the hill that led to Preacher's Cove. They were going to make it.

As Issie and Destiny reached the hill she could see Avery, Kate, Stella, Dan and Ben all mounted on their horses. The riders were in position, their horses almost hidden by the bushes at the top of the ridge next to the fallen tree. The Blackthorn Ponies didn't blink at them as they galloped past. They thundered straight down the road, heading towards the green grass and shady trees at the bottom of the hill.

When the ponies were safely past the fallen tree Issie heard the low rumble of an engine starting up and the graunch of gears and crunch of tyres on the gravel road as Aidan reversed the truck down the hill. As Aidan backed the truck up, manoeuvring it deftly into position, Avery rode forward on Paris and waved directions. Aidan kept driving back until the truck was wedged right in between the steep cliff on one side and the fallen tree on the other. The tree and the truck together created a total road block. The cove was completely closed off now. The only way the Blackthorn Ponies could possibly escape was the same route they took last time – by jumping up and over the fallen tree trunk.

"Tom!" Issie shouted to her instructor. "The tree! They can still hurdle it and get out again."

"Don't worry. We're on it!" Dan yelled out as he and Ben quickly helped Aidan lower the back ramp of the horse truck. The two boys ran inside the truck and emerged carrying a large bundle of what looked like a fishing net. As they unwound the tangled heap and stretched it out, Issie realised it was the old net from the tennis court back at Blackthorn Manor.

Moving quickly, Dan, Ben and Aidan strung the net up – using ropes to attach it to the truck at one end and tying it to the tree roots at the other. The net ran all the way across the top of the fallen tree. It was at least a metre high and bordered by two huge green bands. The ponies would see it quite clearly and there was no way that even the cunning Blackthorn Ponies would manage to jump over this obstacle. They were trapped.

"What happened to you?" Avery had noticed Issie's makeshift sling.

"I'm OK, Tom, honest," Issie insisted. "I can still ride."

Avery looked at her uncertainly.

"Please, Tom. I'm fine. And we don't have time to argue. We still have to get the horses on to the truck."

"All right then," Avery conceded. He turned to the others. "We'll split into two groups. Issie will take Stella and Kate with her down the left-hand side of the cove. I'll ride down the other side with the boys. We'll close in on the herd from either direction, driving them back up the hill. With the tree blocked off now they'll have no choice. They'll have to go up the ramp and on to the truck."

Issie nodded at this and set off down the hill at a canter on Destiny, with Stella and Kate close behind her on Blaze and Nicole. They had almost reached the flat, grassy area at the foot of the hill when Destiny let out a shrill, commanding whinny, calling to his herd.

The buckskin mare responded to his call, nickering back in return.

"Issie, they'll follow Destiny back up the hill. Take

the lead and we'll ride behind you," Stella called to her.

Issie rode Destiny in a sweeping circle, breezing past the buckskin, and the mare instantly picked up the stallion's lead and fell into step behind him, with the other ponies in hot pursuit.

"Excellent! They're following you. Head for the truck!" Avery shouted.

Dust rose up as the ponies cantered back up the dirt road with Issie and Destiny in the lead. At first the noise of the thundering hooves was so loud that Issie didn't notice the four-wheel-drives pulling up at the brow of the hill behind the horse truck. It wasn't until she heard the slamming of car doors and saw Cameron and his men grabbing their rifles and manoeuvring into position along the steep banks of the cliff that she realised what was going on.

"Tom!" Issie cried back over her shoulder.

"I see them," Avery replied. "Don't worry about it; there's nothing they can do. Keep going."

They were just a few metres away from the truck now. Surely the rangers wouldn't shoot and risk hitting one of the riders? Cameron had no choice. He had to give them a chance to get the horses on to the truck.

Issie looked up at the uniformed men who had clambered over the tennis net and were arranging themselves with their guns on the fallen tree. She could see two more rangers climbing up the steep banks to the right, hanging on to tree roots to hoist themselves up with their guns strapped to their backs.

Not much longer now, not much further, Issie thought to herself.

As Issie approached the foot of the ramp she slowed Destiny down to a trot.

"Bring him over here," Aidan instructed, leaping forward to direct her to the side of the ramp.

The rest of the herd had slowed down too and were boggling nervously at the truck.

"Don't give them time to think!" Aidan yelled back at the riders. "Get in behind them now and herd them forward."

"Yee-hah!" There was a cowboy whoop as Ben and Dan rode up on Tornado and Scott, driving the herd forward. The buckskin mare snorted in shock and took a wild leap, cantering up the ramp and into the truck. As she did so, the others followed.

"Keep them moving!" Aidan commanded, bolting the ponies one by one into the partitioned booths in the truck as the boys herded more ponies onboard. Occasionally one would escape their clutches, leaping off the side of the ramp and cantering back down the hill to rejoin the others underneath the trees down by the sea. It was Stella and Kate's job to drive the stragglers up the hill once more to join the herd moving on to the horse truck.

"How many have we got in so far?" Issie shouted out to Aidan.

"Thirteen!" Aidan yelled back. "Do you think we should raise the ramp now?"

Issie nodded. "I guess so. At least that's half of them."

"The rangers are here. We need to move fast," Aidan said. "If we can round the others up and get them penned maybe we can…"

He was interrupted by the sound of screaming.

"What's going on down there?" Avery shouted.

Stella, who had been trying to herd the stragglers back up the hill, was underneath the trees at the far end of the cove. She was trying desperately to hang on to Blaze, but the chestnut mare was going crazy. Stella screamed as Blaze reared straight up in the air, throwing her backwards on to the ground.

"Stella!" Issie began to ride towards her. But instead of looking pleased to see her friend, Stella's face was white with fear as Issie approached.

"Don't!" Stella squealed. "Issie! Stay back!"

Issie was confused. What was wrong? Why didn't Stella want her help?

"In the trees!" Stella yelled. "It's in the trees!"

Issie looked up into the pohutukawa branches above her head. She saw a dark shadow moving, a black blur silhouetted against the blue sky. And then she heard it. The low rumble of the feline growl. So that was what had made Blaze rear!

Issie peered up nervously into the trees above, trying to see where the Grimalkin had gone. She could still hear its growl. She knew it was close.

"Where is it?" Stella said, her eyes flicking nervously over the trees above them. "I don't see it any more. Where is it?"

A bloodcurdling yowl drew their attention from the trees above, followed by the sickening squeal of a horse.

"Blaze!" Issie screamed. The chestnut mare squealed again and gave an enormous buck as a big, black cat the size of a mountain lion leapt on to her back and sunk its claw into her haunches.

Blaze let out a terrified whinny as she felt the claws sink in. She kicked out desperately, trying to free herself from the predator on her back.

"Blaze!" Issie screamed again. She rode Destiny towards the mare. She didn't know what she was going to do, but she did know that she had to try and save her horse.

She had almost reached Blaze when Aidan overtook her on Diablo. "I'll get her. You stay back!" he shouted at Issie as he rode straight at Blaze.

When he reached her he tried to grab the mare by the reins. But Blaze was terrified and bucking like a bronco to get the cat off her back.

With one huge final buck Blaze managed to throw the big cat loose. The Grimalkin turned immediately to new prey, his eyes on Aidan and Diablo. It drew back its lips in a deep, grumbling snarl, revealing a set of long, white fangs.

"Issie, get Stella and Blaze out of here!" Aidan yelled.

"But, Aidan…"

"Do it!" Aidan commanded.

Issie jumped down off Destiny and rushed forward. She had just enough time to pull Stella to her feet before the Grimalkin leapt to attack again. This time the black cat threw itself through the air at Diablo, its gleaming white teeth were bared as it lunged at the horse's neck.

Diablo went up in a half rear to meet the big cat

and just as he did so Issie heard the gun fire. Two shots rang out one after the other, echoing through the cove. Issie turned to see Ranger Cameron perched up on the hill behind them. His face was white with shock. The rifle was raised in his hands.

"Blaze?" Issie yelled, utterly terrified. She ran forward. Where was her horse? In the darkness underneath the trees she could see the body of a horse lying on the ground and as she got closer she felt an icy chill run up her spine.

It was just like her dream. Her heart raced as she reached the point where she saw the horse fall. She was shocked to see not one, but two bodies lying deathly still on the ground.

There was the enormous black shape of the Grimalkin sprawled in front of her, lying there with its deadly jaws spread wide in a rictus smile. Next to the Grimalkin, though, was another body. The body of a horse. It was just like her dream – except she could see now that the horse wasn't Blaze. It was Diablo.

CHAPTER 16

Diablo! Issie ran towards the piebald gelding lying motionless on the ground. She had almost reached the horse's side when she felt strong hands around her shoulders holding her back.

"No, Issie…" Avery said firmly. "It's no use. There's nothing we can do to help him…"

"Tom! Ohmygod! It all happened so fast. I heard the two shots and I thought it was Blaze… and where is Blaze?" Issie was suddenly gripped with panic.

"It's OK. She's here and she's fine. I've got her," Stella called out. "What happened?"

"Cameron shot the Grimalkin – and he shot Diablo too," Issie called back to her.

Dan and Ben had heard the gunshots and were already

off their horses at Issie's side. They stared at the two dark forms on the ground. Dan nervously prodded the limp body of the black cat. Issie could see a trickle of red blood matted into the black fur on its chest where the bullet had entered. The great cat's eyes were shut but its mouth lolled open, exposing two rows of white razor-sharp teeth.

A few metres away from the Grimalkin was the body of Diablo. The horse wasn't moving. Dan gave Diablo a nudge with his foot, but the horse didn't respond.

"Where's Aidan?" Issie suddenly panicked. "He was riding Diablo when he was shot. Where is he now?"

"I'm over here," Aidan called back. He was sitting on the ground under the big pohutukawa tree, looking vacant and dazed.

Issie and Stella ran over to him as Aidan tried to stand up. "I must have been knocked out for a moment," Aidan said, rubbing the back of his head. He still looked wobbly on his feet. "What happened?"

"Diablo's been shot," Issie told him.

"What? But how…"

"Here's Cameron. He knows what happened," Issie said.

"Are you all OK?" Cameron gasped for breath. "I was trying to get a clear shot when I fired at the cat, but there were people in the way and…" Cameron stopped in his tracks when he saw Diablo on the ground. "But… I don't see how… I wasn't aiming for the horse. I was aiming for the cat!" he said. There was a look of horror on his face. "I was aiming for the cat…"

Aidan wasn't listening. He left them standing there and ran over to the horse lying on the ground. His face was ashen as he crouched down beside Diablo and slowly put out his hand to stroke the horse's neck.

"Aidan, I'm so sorry—" Issie began.

Suddenly Aidan leapt back from the horse and stood up. When he turned around to look at the others he had a massive grin on his face.

"Aidan? What is it?" Issie asked.

Aidan looked down at Diablo. "Well done, boy," he said. "Very good!" Then he clapped his hands together twice. "Wake up, Diablo!" he commanded.

On his word, Diablo began to stir, shaking out his mane and snorting as if waking from a nap, pushing himself up on his front legs and then rising on all fours to stand there before them, perfectly and absolutely alive.

"I don't believe it!" Stella was stunned. "You mean he wasn't shot at all?"

"Nope." Aidan couldn't wipe the grin off his face. "He was just performing his favourite trick. He's been trained to pretend that he's dead whenever he hears a gun fire. When Cameron's rifle went off and he fell to the ground you thought he'd been shot, right? But he was just foxing. Weren't you, Diablo?"

"Ohmygod, Diablo!" Issie laughed. "You crazy horse! You scared us all half to death!"

Issie, Stella and Kate all took turns to hug the big piebald while Aidan stood by, stroking Diablo's nose and telling him how clever he was for playing dead.

"I know it gave us all the fright of our lives, but it's exactly what he was trained to do, so I can't tell him off, can I?" Aidan said, grinning. "I'd better go back to the truck and get him a carrot; he deserves a reward for being such a good, dead horse!"

While Aidan raced back to the truck to get Diablo his treat, Avery went to check Blaze's wounds and the riders gathered around the body of the Grimalkin.

"Is *he* really dead?" Stella asked nervously.

Cameron bent down to examine the black cat. He looked back up at Stella and nodded. "I'm afraid so. It looks like one of the bullets went straight through his heart. It would have killed him instantly." Cameron sighed. "It's a terrible shame. I wish I'd had a choice, but when he began to attack Diablo and Aidan I knew I had to shoot…"

Issie looked at the Grimalkin. "He's even bigger than I remember him, that night on the fence behind the stables…"

"He's huge!" Stella agreed. "What sort of animal do you think he is?"

"He looks a bit like a black panther," Ben said, leaning closer and giving the cat a nervous stroke to feel his soft black fur.

"Yes, I think that's exactly right," Cameron said. "Panthera Niger – that's the Latin name for them. They're a type of leopard really – see, underneath the black pigment if you look closely you can make out the spots or rosettes in the fur." Cameron shook his head. "Remarkable! I'd always heard that rumour about one escaping into the hills from that wildlife park a few years back, but I never thought it was true – until now."

"Why did he attack now? Stella asked.

Cameron looked over their heads at the pohutukawa trees.

"Panthers sleep in the trees during the day. He was probably taking a nap and we disturbed him."

"Blaze was so brave fighting him off like that," Stella said.

"Ohmygod, Blaze!" Issie looked over to where Avery was checking the mare's wounds. "I'd better go and see if she's OK."

Avery gave Issie the thumbs up as she headed towards him. "It looks like really good news, Issie," he called out. "A few superficial claw marks and puncture wounds where the cat clung on to her back, but not too bad considering."

Issie gave her pony a hug, wincing a bit as the pain in her arm reminded her of her injured wrist. "Good girl, Blaze! That cat should have known not to mess with you!"

"You see, here," Avery continued, "on her rump… there are a couple of deeper cuts that will need a few stitches. We'll get a vet to come and check on her, but it's nothing to worry about. Blaze is a fighter – she's proven that many times now and she showed it again today. She'll be fine."

"Hey!" Aidan called out to them, "there's still one space in the horse truck, Issie. Blaze is probably a bit too sore to walk all the way back to the manor. She can ride home with the Blackthorn Ponies."

"What about the rest of the ponies?" Kate asked. "We still have ten wild horses trapped in here with us. What are we going to do with them?"

"I think we can help you with that," Cameron said, looking grave as he unslung the gun that was strapped to his back.

"Cameron, please…" Issie began.

The ranger smiled at her. "Don't worry. I don't mean like that, Issie. The cull is cancelled. We have no plans to shoot any more animals today." He turned to his men. "But since we're all here now, I'm sure my rangers would be happy to give you a hand. Do you have a few spare halters in that truck of yours?"

Issie nodded.

"Tell Aidan to keep the truck parked there a little longer and we'll help you to corral the rest of the horses and get halters on them. It'll be easier to get them back to the manor if they're all on lead reins."

"Oh, Cameron, that would be amazing. Thank you!" Issie said.

"Let's get a move on then," Cameron said, "before those ponies in the truck get too restless."

With the help of the rangers it didn't take long at all to catch the stragglers. While the others put halters on the Blackthorn Ponies, Issie was busy loading Blaze into the horse truck.

"Don't worry. She'll be fine. I'll take care of her, I promise," Aidan said. Then he gave the riders a wave and revved the truck into gear, driving off up the Coast Road with the thirteen Blackthorn Ponies and Blaze onboard.

"Are you going to be OK to take it from here?"

Cameron asked Issie as the riders prepared to head home.

"Uh-huh, I think so," Issie said. "We've only got nine Blackthorn ponies left. And six of us. Which would be fine except I can't lead a pony with my wrist in a sling like this. I guess the others are going to have to lead two ponies each."

"I can manage two at once on Diablo," said Avery.

"I think I can take two as well," Kate said.

"So can we," Dan and Ben offered.

"Then I bagsy leading that pretty strawberry roan one if I'm only leading one!" Stella said.

"Ohhh. I was going to choose her," Kate sighed. "All right. I'm having that lovely dapple-grey and the silver roan."

"I'm taking the chestnut with the white star and the buckskin," Ben joined in.

"I'll take the two bays," Dan added.

Avery cocked an eyebrow at them. "I didn't realise we were all picking our favourites. I thought we were herding ponies – not choosing chocolates from a box!"

The riders all laughed. Then they laughed even harder when Avery picked the last two skewbalds in the herd to lead home. "Their patches kind of match yours, don't they, my lad?" he said to Diablo, giving him a slappy pat on his black and white neck.

As the riders tied the ponies' lead ropes to their saddles and prepared to ride out, Cameron strode back over to them. "We're all packed up ready to leave too," he said, gesturing over his shoulder towards his men who were waiting in the jeeps. "I'll call ahead to Hester on the car phone and let her know you're on your way home."

"Thanks, Cameron... for everything." Issie smiled at him.

Cameron smiled back. "You've got some beautiful ponies here, Issie. You did a good job here today."

He turned to Avery. "I hope you'll find good homes for them."

Avery nodded. "The ILPH are already talking to potential owners. We'll get the ponies broken in and schooled up. They're very clever and bold jumpers. The way those ponies jumped that tree the last time we were here, well, I wouldn't be surprised if some of them become eventing superstars one day."

With nine wild horses to manage, the journey home to Blackthorn Manor was a slow ride. By the time the riders came down the long, leafy driveway they were all exhausted. Still, their spirits lifted when they saw the huge banner Hester had painted and strung over the balcony. It read: WELCOME HOME BLACKTHORN PONIES – SAFE AT LAST!

Hester was there waiting for them of course. She was joined on the lawn by a welcoming committee that included Aidan, Nanook, Taxi and Strudel, several of Hester's neighbours and members of the Save the Blackthorn Ponies group, a reporter from the local Gisborne Gazette and a pretty blonde in jodhpurs with a photographer in tow.

The sight of the riders leading the wild ponies down the driveway caused an outbreak of spontaneous clapping from the crowd, and the photographer began to snap furiously like a red-carpet paparazzi trying to get the perfect shot.

"Isadora! Isadora!" the pretty blonde woman with the jodhpurs raced forward. "I'm Cinnamon Lane from *PONY Magazine*. Can I get an exclusive with you about the Blackthorn Ponies? How did you catch them? What will happen now?"

"Cinnamon, dear!" Hester beamed. "I'm sure my niece will be more than happy to give *PONY Magazine* the exclusive story. You're welcome to stay and interview her over dinner. Right now let's get these ponies into the field with the others, get these riders unsaddled and get the kettle on for a nice cup of hot tea. You must all be exhausted!"

It was the best homecoming the riders could have imagined. Down at the stables the riders went out to the paddock to let the new ponies loose and watched as they all happily greeted one another.

"A real family reunion at last!" Hester grinned.

"I can't believe we really saved all of them," Stella said as she leant over the rails to watch the ponies. "They're all together again!"

"Not for long, though," Kate added. "Tom and the ILPH are finding them new homes, remember – they'll have to be split up eventually."

"Well, at least a few of them will be staying together," Hester said. "I've been talking to Tom. He's agreed that Destiny and the two mares with their colts at foot will stay here at Blackthorn Manor with me."

"Really?" Issie said. "Aunty Hess! That's wonderful."

"Well, I couldn't let Avignon's son and his grandchildren go off and live somewhere else now, could I?" Hester said. "Destiny belongs here at Blackthorn

Manor and so do his children. Besides," she added, "I think Tom is right. Those two colts may be future superstars. If they have Avignon's bloodlines and that Blackthorn spirit then there will be no stopping them!"

Issie looked over at Destiny. The black stallion had been put in a separate paddock from the rest of the horses. He was high-stepping now in a swift trot along the fence-line, his head held high. He gave a shrill stallion's call and ran at the fence where Issie was standing, heading straight for her and then swerving at the very last minute with a playful buck.

"Show off!" Issie yelled at him, making Stella and Kate laugh.

"I still can't believe I actually rode him," Issie said softly under her breath.

"I can, my dear." Hester smiled at her. "You're quite the horsewoman. But then, you've got good bloodlines too, you know. I wouldn't expect anything less from my favourite niece." And with that, Hester threw her arms around Issie, smothering her once more in a tight, Chanel-scented hug.

CHAPTER 17

It turned out that Issie's arm was badly sprained, but thankfully not broken.

"Thank goodness! Your mother would have killed me if I'd sent you home in a cast," Hester said. "Still, I don't suppose she'll be any more pleased when you turn up wearing that bandage and a sling."

Issie was hoping that the last few days at the farm would have been enough time for her arm to heal before she had to face her mother. But the doctor said she needed to keep wearing the sling for another week – and it was time to go home.

"The holidays are over and my leg is on the mend. I'll be getting the cast off next week," said Aunt Hester. "I've called your mother and she's expecting you home tomorrow. Tom is going to borrow my horse float to take Blaze back with you too. You can leave as soon as she's had her vet check in the morning."

"I can't believe I'm going to be leaving," Issie said. "I love it here so much. And I'll miss you, Aunty Hess."

"Well of course you will, darling! But you'll come back again, won't you? Blackthorn Manor is your home too now."

Dinner that night was a celebration and a farewell. All the riders had helped in the kitchen so that Aunt Hester could have a night off cooking. "This is the best meal I've ever had at Blackthorn Manor!" Aidan said as he tucked into a perfect piece of roast beef and mashed potato.

That night, for the last time, Issie went to sleep staring at the painting of Avignon opposite her enormous four-poster bed. When she woke up the next morning Strudel was sniffing around her feet and the sun was streaming in through the windows.

Issie had already packed her bags the night before. Now, as she pulled on her jersey and jeans, she decided to say goodbye one last time to the manor menagerie before breakfast. In the kitchen she found a bag of carrots to take with her as a goodbye treat for Butch, Blossom and the rabbits, throwing in a few apples as well as a farewell gift for the ponies.

The early morning light was golden and warm as she walked across the lawn. The rest of the house was shrouded in sleep and the air was still. She stopped off to see Butch, feeding the greedy pig four big carrots, then walked on past the duck pond to Destiny's paddock.

Issie was surprised when the stallion didn't hesitate, but came straight up to the fence to greet her. As the horse poked his elegant neck over the rails of the fence to take a carrot Issie put out a hand to stroke his glossy, jet mane.

"We would never have saved the ponies without you, Destiny," she said softly. Destiny gave a nicker as if he understood. Issie was about to say something else when a low, feline growl behind her made her jump.

"Meow!" Aidan grinned. "I can't believe you're still falling for that old trick, Issie!"

"Aidan!" Issie scowled at him. "I knew you weren't the Grimalkin – you just startled me, that's all."

"Sorry," Aidan said. Although he didn't look sorry at all. He was still smiling as he came over to the fence, took a carrot out of Issie's bag and fed it to a buckskin mare who had finally summoned up the courage to come close enough to the railing.

"Do you think they'll be OK? The Blackthorn Ponies, I mean," Issie said to Aidan.

"Yeah, I do. They'll be just fine – thanks to you," Aidan said.

"Me? No… I didn't do anything…"

"Of course you did," Aidan said. "You were amazing, Issie…" Aidan went quiet and looked at his feet. "Listen, I've been trying to tell you something since the first day you got here." Aidan's bright blue eyes were almost hidden beneath his black fringe as he looked up at her.

"What is it?" Issie asked.

"This," Aidan said. And without another word he stepped forward and kissed her.

Issie felt her heart skip a beat as Aidan's lips brushed against her own. Then she jumped back in shock. "You kissed me!" she said.

"I know!" Aidan said. "I was hoping that, well, that you wouldn't mind."

"I don't… it's just, well, I'm just kind of surprised…" Issie felt the butterflies in her tummy fluttering like crazy. Aidan had just kissed her!

"I didn't mean to… I… I'd better go…" Aidan said, his face glowing with embarrassment.

"No! Don't!" Issie yelled after him. But it was too late.

Aidan was already racing off back across the lawn towards the manor. She was about to run after him when a voice from the stable doorway startled her.

"Isadora! There you are!" Tom Avery called to her. "I've been looking for you everywhere. The vet has some very important news about Blaze. You'd better come in here immediately."

The warmth of Aidan's kiss disappeared as if someone had poured ice water all over her. Issie broke into a run and followed Avery back in through the stable door to the very last stall in the row where Blaze's nameplate was now hung from the carved wooden horse head on the door. Inside the stall the vet was bending over the mare. He had a syringe of blood in his hand and a worried expression on his face.

"What's wrong with Blaze. What is that for?" Issie asked, looking at the vial of blood that the vet was now putting into a plastic bag in his hold-all.

"This must be the mare's owner, yes?" the vet said to Avery.

"Yes, Andrew, this is Isadora. You'd better tell her what you just told me."

Issie felt the blood drain from her face. "Tom? What is it? What's wrong with Blaze? What is all this about?

I thought you said her wounds weren't that bad. She just needed stitches…"

Issie was panicking now; she could feel her heart racing. She felt like she was going to be sick.

"Isadora, no! I'm sorry. I've gone and given you the wrong end of the stick here." Avery smiled. "Blaze is just fine, but, well, you'd better explain Andrew…"

The vet stepped forward. "I came in to treat your mare this morning and when I was checking her wounds I noticed a few things about her that seemed odd. I've given her a thorough check-up, and I'm pretty sure that I'm right. I've taken blood tests which will confirm it once I've got them back to the lab but in the meantime you just need to make sure she's well fed. Just treat her normally and she should be…"

"I'm sorry… you still haven't told me… what is wrong with my horse?" Issie couldn't stand it any longer. "What is the matter with Blaze?"

"Nothing's wrong with her," the vet said. "Your horse isn't sick, Issie, she's in foal."

"In foal? You mean Blaze is going to have a baby?"

"It certainly looks likely," the vet said, popping the last of his equipment into the hold-all and giving Blaze a pat. "Your mare is about to become a mummy."

"Blaze!" Issie squealed, throwing her arms around the mare's neck. "Ohmygod! That's wonderful!"

The news that Blaze was in foal came as such a shock to Issie that the drive home to Chevalier Point was a total blur. She was so overcome, she didn't know what to think. Blaze, her own special pony, was going to have a foal!

"Isn't this the most exciting news you've ever heard in your whole life!" Stella squealed in the back seat of the Range Rover where the three girls were crammed in together.

"Can you still ride her?" Ben asked. He and Dan were sitting up the front with Avery for the ride home.

"The vet said it was fine – at least until her tummy gets really big," Issie nodded.

"And Destiny is the father, right?" Kate said.

Issie shook her head. "The vet couldn't tell me that for sure. He needs to check the blood tests first. I guess we'll know in a day or two."

"Ohmygod! Imagine how beautiful the foal is going to be!" Kate beamed. "What do you think she'll have, Issie? A filly or a colt?"

"I hope it's a girl," Stella said. "A little baby Blaze running around. How cute would that be?"

For the whole trip they talked on and on about the foal, what it would look like and what they were going to name it. Issie was so excited, she almost forgot all the other events of the past few weeks: breaking in Destiny, making the Flying Angel leap from Mystic, saving the Blackthorn Ponies and her kiss with Aidan that morning...

It was late afternoon when the Range Rover pulled up at the pony club. Avery pulled the horse float to a stop underneath the magnolia trees in the first paddock and Stella jumped out to help Issie lower the tail flap.

"Here, you can't do that with your sore wrist. I'll help you put Blaze's rug on while you get the feed sorted," Stella told Issie.

"Thanks," Issie said.

"How much longer are you going to have that sling for anyway?"

"The doctor said maybe a week or so. It's starting to feel better already." She gave her wrist a wiggle.

When Issie emerged again from the tack room with Blaze's feed the mare was rugged up and ready for her.

"I'm going to check on Coco. I'll meet you back at the

car," Stella told Issie, leaving her alone with her pony.

Blaze shoved her head eagerly into the feed bucket, then lifted it up again and gave a happy nicker across the paddock, calling out to Coco and Toby.

"It's good to be home again, huh, girl?" Issie said.

She was just waiting for Blaze to chew up the last remnants of her chaff and pony nuts when she saw a rider striding towards her from the clubrooms. Even at a distance she recognised the stiff blonde plaits and haughty manner immediately.

"Hello, Natasha," Issie sighed as the rider approached her.

"Isadora! I thought it was you," Natasha said icily. "Mummy just brought me to the club to pick up my hard hat. I left it behind at training. And here you are! Well, I must say I'm so glad you're back!"

"Really?" Issie looked at her.

"Yes. I wanted you to be the first to congratulate me on my win," Natasha smirked.

"What?" Issie was confused.

"The summer dressage series. I completely won it. Fabergé and I annihilated the competition. Nobody else stood a chance!" Natasha's smirk had spread from ear to ear now. "Of course I know that technically you didn't compete because you weren't here, but I can tell you that Fabby was pretty unbeatable. I'm sure that we would have won anyway, even if you had been riding. So that makes us the best in the whole club. Anyway," Natasha looked over at the Range Rover where Stella and Kate were staring at her through the windows, "I see you're all back. How was your holiday? Did anything interesting happen?"

Issie looked back at Stella and Kate, who were now pulling faces at Natasha and mouthing at Issie to hurry up.

"Nope," Issie said with a grin on her face. "I mean, what can I say that could possibly beat your story, Natasha? Wow, huh? Good for you! It sounds like you've had quite the exciting time. I'd love to hear more about it, but I need to put Blaze in her paddock and get home now. It's been a long day."

Issie tried to suppress her giggles as she turned away from Natasha and led Blaze through the paddock gate. She didn't need to tell Stuck-up Tucker about what had happened. Natasha would no doubt hear all about it at the pony club soon enough.

Issie slipped the halter off Blaze's head and watched as the mare trotted off happily to join Coco and Toby. It was hard to believe that her pony was going to have a foal.

"I hope it's a girl. She'll be beautiful, Blaze – just like you," Issie said.

As Avery leant on the horn of the Range Rover, telling her to hurry up, Issie paused and took another look around the familiar fields of the Chevalier Point Pony Club. It was good to be home.

Don't miss

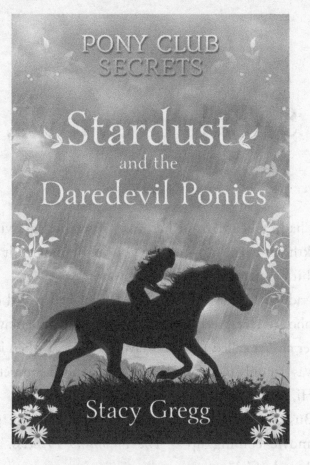

PONY CLUB
SECRETS

Stardust
and the
Daredevil Ponies

Stacy Gregg

Issie has landed her dream job – handling
horses on a real film set.

But what is spoilt star Angelique's big secret?
Could this be Issie's chance for stardom?

HarperCollins *Children's Books*

Sneak preview...

Issie hadn't heard from her aunt since her last visit to Blackthorn Farm so when she got the phone call it came as a bit of surprise.

"Isadora! My favourite niece!" Hester had trilled down the phone. Her greeting made Issie laugh straightaway – Hester always called Issie her "favourite niece" when in fact she was her only niece so she didn't have much competition!

"Hi, Aunty Hess. How are things at the farm?"

"Busy, busy, busy!" Hester told her. "We've got a big movie coming up – *The Palomino Princess*. Have you heard of it?"

"Ohmygod!" Issie squealed. "Aunty Hess! I love that book! Are they making a film of it? How cool! And your horses are going to be in it?"

"Absolutely," Hester said. "Well, at least a few of

them are – Paris and Nicole and Destiny and Diablo to be exact. They need quite a few stunt horses for the film, as you'll know if you've already read the books. Paris and Nicole are perfect for princess horses, and Diablo is having his piebald patches dyed so that he can play one of the pitch-black Horses of Darkness."

"That's so exciting!" Issie said.

"I'm glad you think so, dear," Hester said, "because I was hoping you might want to come and work with me on the movie."

"What? Me?"

"Well, yes. And your friends too. They're looking for riders and wranglers right now and you've got some school holidays coming up. I thought the timing was perfect," Hester said.

"I couldn't…" Issie began to protest, but Hester interrupted.

"I know Blaze is expecting her foal and you won't want to leave her alone," Hester said, "but the movie set isn't far away from Chevalier Point. You could still go home on weekends to check on her. How long is it now until she's due?"

"The vet says she has maybe a month to go," Issie said.

"Well, that's perfect then! Filming will be wrapped by the time the foal arrives. And you've got nothing better to do in your holidays since you can't ride her now. She'll be so fat you won't be able to fit a girth around that tummy of hers!" Hester said.

"Listen, my favourite niece, I could really do with your help. There are nearly two dozen horses in this film and Aidan and I are responsible for all of them. It's proving tricky to find riders who are the right size to play the palomino princesses. We need four girls who fit the costumes to double for the stars of the film, and they must be good riders. They can't be too grown-up. Princess Galatea and her riders are all, well, actually they're about your size…" Hester paused. "We'll pay you all, of course– film rates for stunt riders are really good."

"It all sounds great, Aunty Hess!" Issie said. "And I'm sure Stella and Kate will be keen, and we can find a fourth girl to ride with us…"

"Excellent!" Hester said. "So what's the best way to organise this? Do you want to put your mother on the phone? I think she's more likely to say yes if I ask her, don't you?"

"Actually, Aunty Hess, I wouldn't bet on it. She's still mad at you after last time," Issie said.

"Oh, I was hoping she would have forgotten about that by now," Hester said.

The last time Issie had stayed with her aunt she had returned home with her arm in sling – a fact that her mother was none too happy about.

"Your mum is such a fuss-pot," Hester sighed. "It was only a little sprain. Put her on the phone. I'm sure she'll say yes once I talk her round."

"Muuum!" Issie called with her hand over the receiver. "It's for you!"

As Mrs Brown took the phone out of her daughter's hands with a quizzical look Issie held her breath and hoped Aunt Hester would be able to make her mother say yes.

Issie's mum and Aunt Hester were sisters – but the two women were the complete opposite of each other in every way. Hester was, as she put it, a "bit too bohemian for her own good". She had been an actress before she gave up the movies herself and started training animals to act instead.

Issie could hear her mum on the phone now with Aunty Hess and it sounded like Hester was getting a telling-off. She could only catch snippets of the conversation but it clearly wasn't going well.

"…Hester! You must be joking!" she heard her mum say. "…Safe? What do you mean safe? Last time she came home with her arm in a sling… No, it's far too dangerous…"

Issie slunk away to the kitchen and waited for her mum

to finish yelling at Hester and get off the phone. Finally she heard the receiver being hung up and Mrs Brown appeared in the kitchen doorway, her arms crossed in front of her, and her brow furrowed in a deep frown.

"I have a feeling that you already know what that phone call was about," she said.

"Uh-huh," Issie said.

"So you really want to help Hess with this movie?" Mrs Brown said.

"Uh-huh."

Mrs Brown sighed. "I've told Hester that if I see so much as a sticky plaster on you when you come home this time I will hold her responsible. She insists that it's perfectly safe. There's a bit of riding, apparently, but you'll mostly just be grooming the horses and mucking out the stalls."

"Wait a minute!" Issie said. "Does that mean you're going to let me go?"

Mrs Brown nodded. "Your Aunty Hess is very convincing. You start work as a stunt rider on *The Palomino Princess* next Monday."

To be continued...